THE CAMP FIRE GIRLS
BEHIND THE LINES

MARGARET VANDERCOOK

The Camp Fire Girls Behind The Lines

CHAPTER I

"EL CAMINO REAL"

A small cavalcade was slowly winding down a steep, white road.

The bare, brown hills rose up on one side like the earth's friars of St. Francis, while on the other, at some distance away, the Pacific Ocean showed green and still. Near the shore the waves broke into white sprites of foam against the deep, incurving cliffs.

A girl riding at the head of the column reined in her horse, afterwards making a mysterious sign in the air with one upraised hand.

In answer to her signal the other riders, a group of Camp Fire girls, also stopped their horses. Across many miles sounded faintly the deep-toned voices of old mission bells.

"I believe the mission is ringing a farewell to us," one of the girls remarked to the companion whose western pony had stopped nearest her own. "To me, of all the Spanish missions we have seen so far, Carmel was the loveliest. 'Carmelo' — why, the very name has an enchanting sound!

"Bells of the Past, whose long-forgotten musicStill fills the wide expanse,Tingeing the sober twilight of the PresentWith colors of romance!

"I hear you call, and see the sun descendingOn rock and wave and sand,As down the coast the mission voices, blending,Girdle the heathen land!

"Borne on the swell 'of your long waves receding,I touch the farther Past — I see the dying glow of Spanish glory,The sunset dream and last!"

The girl who had been reciting possessed an odd, charming voice with a slightly hoarse note. She was small and had bright, almost copper-colored hair. Her slender nose, which had a queer little twist at the end, destroyed any claim she might otherwise have had to conventional beauty and yet curiously enough added to the fascination of her expression.

The other girl shook her head.

"I don't agree with you, Marta. You seem to me in as great a state of enthusiasm over everything we have seen in California as if you were a native. I confess to you I am a little weary of visiting old Spanish missions. Personally I shall be glad when we are in our summer camp. The missions are so empty and so sleepy these days with their queer, dreamy old gardens and no one to be seen except an occasional tourist and a few old monks. Nevertheless I liked your recitation. Sometimes I wonder, Marta, if you intend imitating our Camp Fire guardian's career?"

Gerry Williams spoke in a voice of amused superiority she often employed in talking with other girls.

Marta Clark's eyes, which had the strange characteristic of appearing to change in color according to her moods, now darkened slightly as she turned to gaze steadily at her companion.

"Do you know, Gerry, I have an idea the old missions would never have bored you, if you had any thought that a prince might come and discover you in one of them!"

"Certainly not," Gerry laughed.

Gerry was alluring. Her hat was hanging over the pommel of her saddle so that her fair hair was blowing about her face. Now that the sun and wind had tanned her delicate skin, her blue eyes looked bluer than ever.

Instead of replying, Marta Clark, at this instant, turned her horse with the intention of riding beside one of the other girls.

Marta Clark was the latest addition to the new group of Sunrise Hill Camp Fire girls. The summer before she had met them in Arizona where they were camping at the "End of the Trail." At that time she was living nearby in a tent with her brother who had been seriously ill. Her brother's health had improved and he had written a successful play. Afterwards his marriage to Ellen Deal, one of the older Camp Fire girls, had made it possible for Marta Clark to accept Mrs. Burton's invitation to join her Camp

Fire group. As her guests they were now traveling along the Pacific coast, visiting the old Spanish missions.

The King's Highway, called in the old Spanish tongue, El Camino Real, stretches from northern California to the southernmost end.

One of the other Camp Fire girls turned her head as Marta came near her. All the horses were moving on again.

"I wonder why the automobile has not caught up with us?" Peggy Webster remarked. "I supposed the car would have passed us long ago. As it is time for tea, and I am already tired, I think it would have been more sensible if we had remained together."

The little riding party of six girls was accompanied by a large wagon filled with a camping outfit. The wagon was drawn by a small pair of gray mules and driven by a tall, raw-boned man, a typical western plainsman. Beside him sat a young fellow about seventeen years old. The wagon was following a few yards behind the riders.

"Then suppose we stop and have tea while we wait and watch for the others," Bettina Graham proposed, having overheard Peggy's lament.

"I don't believe they could have lost their way, since one has only to follow the guide posts of the old mission bells. Nevertheless Tante has a most eccentric fashion of suddenly deciding to explore along small byways. But they must surely come along here finally."

Peggy Webster shook her head.

"We had best ride on for a little while longer in order to make the distance we planned to make today. Perhaps by that time the car will have joined us. In any case we can find a better place to watch and to prepare tea."

At the present time on each side the road the mustard plants were blooming, making a broad field of the cloth of gold broken only by the long trail.

4

Further along down the slope of a hillside a miniature orange grove had been planted with trees no larger than would have comfortably shaded dolls' houses.

Then, as they rode on, the Camp Fire girls drew nearer to the fine of the coast. A fog was blowing in from the sea.

Finally, standing up in her stirrups for an instant, Peggy Webster pointed ahead.

"See those three rocks down there that look like 'the Big Bear, the Middle-Sized Bear and the Little Bear,' in the fairy story! Don't you think they would form a comfortable background for our tea party? At least they will be a protection from the wind. If we go on and the fog grows much thicker we shall not be able even to see each other."

Soon after the horses and the wagon halted and Dan Webster climbed down, bearing the tea basket. Mr. Simpson, who was continuing to act as guide, took charge of the horses.

The coast looked bare and wind-swept. There were no trees nearby and no driftwood along the shore.

However, nearly two hundred years before, when Father Juniper Serra founded and built the Spanish missions of California, he and his brother monks left behind them a golden harvest. In all their pilgrimages from land's end to land's end they flung the seed of the mustard plant along their route.

Leaving the other girls to unpack the tea basket, Marta Clark and Bettina walked quickly back along the road until not a quarter of a mile away they discovered another field of the omnipresent mustard.

Then the two girls began searching for the dried stems of the mustard plant in order to start their camp fire.

Bettina was standing with her arms filled with the long stems when Marta Clark came close up beside her. Both of the girls were knee deep among the golden flowers.

"You look like Ruth among the corn, Bettina," Marta remarked, surveying the other girl with generous admiration.

"Do you remember the story of Ruth in the Bible? 'So she gleaned in the field until even, and beat out that she had gleaned. And she took it up and went into the city.'"

Bettina shook her head. "No, I do not remember. It is wonderful to me, your ability to quote so correctly. If ever you are able to do the thing you desire, your memory will be a wonderful help. But I am not going to talk about it. I know you feel as embarrassed over your ambition as I do over mine."

In the past few weeks Marta Clark and Bettina were beginning to feel a deep interest in each other. This was but natural, for although they were unlike in character they had many tastes in common. Marta was quick and passionate, while Bettina was apt to appear almost too serene and self-controlled. Yet they both cared for books, for human beauty and the beauty of the great outdoors.

During the few moments the girls were talking the fog had been closing in more thickly about them until it was only possible to see the road a few yards away through a cloak of mist.

At this instant they distinctly heard the noise of an approaching motor car.

Mrs. Richard Burton, better known to the world as the famous actress, Polly O'Neill Burton, and guardian to the group of Sunrise Hill Camp Fire girls, had chosen to make the journey down the California coast in her automobile.

This afternoon her sister, Mrs. Webster, her nephew, Billy Webster, Vera Lagerloff and the maid, Marie, were traveling with her.

The plan had been that the Camp Fire girls should start on their riding trip several hours ahead and that they meet later and camp for the night at some agreeable place along their journey.

Marta and Bettina ran forward, intending to stop the approaching car. Both girls were thinking that the car was moving much more swiftly than usual.

Almost immediately they saw that the automobile coming toward them was not Mrs. Burton's, but a small khaki-colored roadster driven by a United States officer with another soldier on the seat beside him.

They were going along at full speed as if they were carrying information of great importance.

Then suddenly, without Marta or Bettina recognizing the cause, the car swerved, made a wide detour and quickly overturned. A few seconds later when the two girls, hoping to be of service, had reached the car, the young United States officer was crawling slowly out from beneath the wreck.

He tried to stand up and to smile reassuringly at Bettina, who chanced to be ahead, but the next moment if she had not put out her arm to steady him he would have fallen.

A little while after he was sitting unheroically amid the dust of the roadside, smiling somewhat quizzically up at his rescuer.

"I don't believe I am seriously hurt," he remarked cheerfully, "but as I know you are patriotic and would like to try your first-aid remedies upon me, please go ahead. I am Lieutenant Carson and at present I appear to be a somewhat unsuccessful Paul Revere. But would you mind explaining, while you are washing the dirt out of this plagued cut on my forehead, why you are wearing a costume that seems to suggest a combination of an Indian princess' outfit and a soldier's uniform?"

Marta Clark was devoting her attention to the other soldier, who did not appear to be hurt but only slightly dazed from his mishap.

Bettina for an instant regretted that she was unable to change places with Marta. She had studied first aid, of course, along with her Camp Fire work, but was not accustomed to masculine patients.

Moreover, Bettina considered that the young officer was showing an unwarranted personal interest in his first war nurse. As a matter of fact, she entirely refused to pay any attention to his questioning.

CHAPTER II

THE LAND OF ROMANCE

Two weeks later two women were walking up and down a garden path in the moonlight.

Across from them stood a long, low adobe house of a single story. The veranda, extending from one end to the other, was so thickly covered with a flowering vine that even in the moonlight one could get the reflection of its brilliant color. The air was scented with the fragrant perfume of roses and the blossoms of orange and lemon trees. From behind the soft shading of the vine across the road came the brilliant twanging of a guitar and a mandolin. Two voices were singing a Spanish love song.

Farther away under the deeper shadow of the moon a white cross arose above a mass of fallen stone.

"I declare, Mollie, this is the old world, not the new, isn't it? I feel as if we had traveled away from our own country today into a foreign land; but what land I cannot say, because this place tonight must be more beautiful and more romantic than even Spain itself. Yet one is not sorry to forget for a little while the present world and its tragedies!"

The other woman shook her head. The two sisters were the same height, had nearly the same character of features and the same coloring; nevertheless were curiously unlike.

One conspicuous difference was in their voices.

"Do you know, Polly, I think perhaps you have made a mistake in bringing the Camp Fire girls to spend the summer in so picturesque a place. We probably shall have a romance on our hands before the season is over," Mrs. Webster answered. "It is natural of course that you should be affected by such surroundings. But when a night like this has an influence upon a woman of my age with an almost grown-up family, it makes me feel extremely nervous when I consider the girls."

Mrs. Burton laughed.

"Nevertheless, my beloved Mollie, even if you have a grown-up family and I have no children, I don't see what difference the fact makes in our ages, as we happen to be twins. Besides, I never could see why age should destroy one's susceptibility to beauty! My only feeling is that perhaps we have no right to ease and enjoyment of any kind this summer, now that the United States has entered the war. I don't think I should have invited the girls on this long trip had I known beforehand. I feel I ought to be devoting all my energies to war work; however, we must do whatever we can out here. Richard seemed to think it impossible to have me near the southern camp where he is located."

Mrs. Webster sighed gently in response. She was unhappy over the war, too, but not so inclined as her sister to take deeply to heart the sorrows of the world when they did not touch her personally.

"Well, I am glad we can be together for a few months longer, Polly. I realize it is selfish of me, and yet I do rejoice that neither Dan nor Billy is old enough to be drafted. Dan's desire to volunteer is of course ridiculous! At least, I shall safe-guard my boys. I am also glad my husband is doing war work by increasing the amount of food raised upon our place, instead of entering the service as an ordnance officer as your husband has. Dear me, I really think it is very fine of Richard at his age!"

Shrugging her shoulders, Mrs. Burton smiled a little ruefully.

"You are determined to dwell upon our great age tonight, aren't you, Mollie mine? Please remember that your daughter Peggy bestowed her affections upon Ralph Marshall last summer when we were at the Grand Canyon and not in southern California. Yet I do feel that with the possibility of young soldiers and officers turning up at any moment in our midst, you and I will have to be unusually vigilant chaperons.

"But do let us go now and find what has become of the girls. We have had a long journey and should soon be in bed."

Mrs. Burton slipped her arm inside her sister's and drew her away from the old hotel garden across the gleaming road.

To the right of them, bathed in the half-tropic moonlight, was the old Spanish mission of San Juan Capistrano, named in honor of a warrior-saint of the Crusades. It was the loveliest place in all California.

As they walked slowly on Mrs. Burton recited in an undertone, and with the emotional sweetness which had captivated countless audiences and which never failed to thrill her sister:

"Up from the south slow filed a train,Priests and soldiers of old Spain,Who through the sunlit country woundWith cross and lance, intent to foundA mission in that wild to John,Soldier saint of Capistran."

They stopped a moment as if to let the beauty sink deep, and then the two women entered the gate of the old mission grounds.

Early in the afternoon the Sunrise Camp Fire party had arrived at the little half-foreign town of Capistrano, set midway, like a link with the past, between the two modern cities of San Diego and Los Angeles. For hours they had been exploring the old mission. Then, after dinner, the Camp Fire girls, with Dan and Billy Webster to act as escorts had asked the privilege of returning to remain in the old mission garden until bedtime.

Tonight, to Mrs. Burton's eyes at least, the mission looked like a half-ruined palace of dreams. Once the mission of San Juan Capistrano held a great stone church, a pillared court, a portico, a rectangle; here the Franciscan fathers had their cells, and many rooms for distinguished guests. It was the richest and most splendid mission in old California.

But at present only the ruins of its past remained.

Above, in one of the crumbling arches of the colonnade, an owl hooted so hoarsely that Mrs. Webster clutched her sister's arm in a tighter clasp. The greeting had sounded, not like a welcome, but a warning.

There was no one to be seen and the place was wrapped in a kind of ghostly silence.

"It is most extraordinary how the girls and Dan and Billy have disappeared," Mrs. Burton whispered plaintively, scarcely daring to speak in a natural tone.

She and Mrs. Burton had passed through one of the colonnades and were now in the old court in the rear. Along one side ran a line of forsaken cloisters.

"Wait a moment, Mollie, please," Mrs. Burton murmured.

Adding to the enchantment of the present scene she could hear again the sound of music. The two musicians who had been singing on the veranda across from their hotel also must have wandered into the mission grounds.

Then, almost at the same instant, Mrs. Burton and Mrs. Webster discovered the Camp Fire girls.

Beyond the enclosed space of the old mission lay a broad piece of open ground. Over it tonight poured the unbroken radiance of the moon. In time long past this ground had been devoted to the use of the Indians who were being taught Christianity and the habits of civilization by the Spanish fathers. In those days this ground was encircled by a row of Indian huts. One part was set apart for the Indian women and girls, and here the Indian maiden remained in seclusion until her wedding day.

But tonight, in some mysterious fashion, the past seemed to have came back, for a group of Indian maidens had returned to their former dwelling place.

"The picture is too lovely to disturb," Mrs. Burton whispered irresolutely.

In the moonlight one could not discern the differences in the costumes of the Camp Fire girls, nor their fairer coloring.

Bettina, Marta, Peggy and Alice Ashton were seated upon the ground, forming a square, with Dan standing apparently hovering like a guardian angel above them.

As usual, Billy Webster was lying gazing up at the sky and Vera Lagerloff was sitting beside him.

A little apart from the others Gerry Williams and Sally Ashton were strolling up and down with their arms intertwined.

"Do you think we should speak of our plan immediately?" Bettina Graham was inquiring of the other three girls. "Unless we can carry it out I don't feel that we have the right to our Camp Fire summer together."

In the moonlight her yellow brown hair had turned a bright gold.

Peggy, who was ever a direct and sensible person, shook her head.

"We must wait until we have found the location for our camp and are fairly well settled," she replied. "At present our own ideas as to what we can do to help with the war work are much too vague. But I suppose we shall be near the great National Guard war training camp, and that in itself ought to be an inspiration. Have you ever heard from your wounded lieutenant, Bettina? It was amusing to have him and his friend to tea in so unexpected a fashion. I shall never forget how amazed the family was on discovering us with soldier guests. I am sorry we have never seen either of them again."

"I have had one note from Lieutenant Carson, saying that he was all right," Bettina answered. "He will probably be stationed at the cantonment near here. I wish for your sake Ralph Marshall was to be there instead."

There was no engagement existing between Peggy Webster and Ralph Marshall. But Peggy was too transparent a person to conceal her interest in Ralph after their past summer of misunderstanding and final reconciliation. As Ralph had volunteered and joined the aviation corps soon after the entry of the United States into the war, she had not seen him in many months. But it was understood that they wrote to each other and Peggy openly expressed her pride in Ralph's courage and ability. Ralph had been offered an opportunity to remain in his own country and act as an aviation instructor, but instead had chosen to go to France. At the present time he was in a camp on Long Island waiting his hour for sailing.

Before Peggy could make a reply to Bettina's final speech, the four girls saw their Camp Fire guardians approaching and rose to greet them.

"You girls look too picturesque to disturb, and yet we must not remain outdoors all night, no matter how the beauty of the night tempts us. I trust we may have many other nights as radiant as this before our summer is over," said Mrs. Burton, half apologizing for her own and her sister's intrusion.

A few moments later the Sunrise Camp Fire girls were walking slowly away from the mission grounds to their own rose-covered hotel.

Not by accident, but because of a common purpose, Sally and Gerry managed to linger a few yards behind the others.

The singing which had so fascinated Mrs. Burton and added to the witchery of the night had also attracted the attention of the two girls. But it was not the music alone which had charmed them. In their careless strolling up and down apart from their companions, Sally and Gerry had dimly seen the figures of the two musicians.

The mysterious singers had kept always in the background, only approaching sufficiently near for their songs to be heard; and yet, notwithstanding this, Sally and Gerry had managed to find out that they were two young men dressed in Mexican costumes. But whether they were Mexicans or Americans they could not guess, since it was impossible to see their faces and they seemed able to sing Spanish or English songs with equal ease.

The fact was that Gerry and Sally had arranged a scheme between them by which they hoped to make a desired discovery. Their scheme would have appalled the other Camp Fire girls, but they chanced to have unlike views in regard to the agreeable adventures and experiences of life. Moreover, they often preferred bestowing their confidences only upon each other.

As the rest of the Camp Fire party moved on, both Sally and Gerry became aware that the musicians were growing bolder and were drawing nearer.

Both girls would have liked to turn round and deliberately look back. Yet they had scarcely the courage for this breach of taste, in spite of the fact that it was night and the redeeming grace of the moonlight rested over them.

Sally was carrying a little beaded Indian bag which she managed to drop without any one, aside from Gerry, noticing.

After going on a little further, unexpectedly they turned back to pick up the lost possession.

The two young men were thus within only a few feet of them.

There was but little satisfaction in the adventure, nevertheless, for although one of the musicians stepped forward and gravely presented Sally with the Indian bag he had observed on the ground between them; yet neither he nor his companion spoke and it was impossible, with their broad Mexican hats, to obtain a satisfactory view of their faces without revealing too great curiosity.

As a matter of fact, the entire Camp Fire party was unaware of the interest their appearance in the little town of Capistrano during the afternoon had excited. There were always tourists visiting the old mission, especially at this season of the year. But the number and appearance of the girls, their picturesque, half Indian costumes, which always puzzled people unacquainted with the Camp Fire uniform, and the big wagon carrying their large camping outfit, gave them a unique distinction.

CHAPTER III

THE CALL TO SERVICE

On a ledge of rock with the Pacific Ocean as a background a girl was standing, holding a bugle to her lips and with it sounding a clear, musical call.

Not far off a number of persons were seated about a smouldering camp fire. All day the sun had been hot, almost as a tropic sun, but now with the coming of the late afternoon a cool breeze was blowing in from the sea.

The feminine members of the little circle were knitting and sewing.

One of the two young men was holding a hank of wool, which a brown-haired, brown-eyed girl was winding slowly and carefully into a great ball. The other was lying full length on the ground looking toward the water.

"Why is my Sister Peggy sounding taps or a reveille, since at present it is neither morning nor night?" he questioned. "It seems impossible these days to get away from the sights and sounds which suggest war. I had hoped that when we were in camp out here in this far-away country we might at least have a little rest."

Billy Webster's manner was that of a spoiled and fretful boy; nevertheless an uncomfortable silence followed his speech.

Ever it appears impossible in this world, even among a small group of persons, to preserve entire harmony! In spite of his youth and his fragility, in spite of his quiet voice and oftentimes gentle manner, Billy Webster, from the time he ceased wearing dresses, had been able to sow discord. The trouble was that Billy always refused to think like the people surrounding him.

At present, when the entire Camp Fire party was interested heart and soul in the successful carrying on of the war, Billy had announced himself a pacifist. If he had contented himself with the mere announcement, his friends and family would have accepted his point of view with comparative equanimity. But with Billy the frequent exposition of his opinions was as the breath of life.

At this moment Vera Lagerloff leaned over to say in a whisper:

"For goodness' sake, Billy, please don't start an argument now on the subject of the war. You know how intensely Mrs. Burton disapproves of your ideas and how angry you make Dan."

Peggy descended from her rocky platform at this instant and joined the group. She was wearing her workaday Camp Fire costume and had her dark hair braided in two braids with a red band about her forehead.

"What is it, Peggy? You look as if you had something important to confide to us?" Mrs. Burton asked quickly, hoping to stem the flood of eloquence with which her nephew ordinarily met opposition. "I confess I am as curious as Billy to know why you sounded a bugle call at this hour of the afternoon."

Peggy sat down in camp-fire fashion on the ground, frowning and looking extremely serious. A bunch of pale lavender sea verbena she had gathered nearer the shore, she dropped in her mother's lap.

She did not know what Billy had been saying, but she was conscious that the atmosphere about her was uncomfortable.

Dan had not moved from his patient attitude, in order that Sally Ashton might continue to unwind her wool, yet his expression was not like his usual sweet-tempered one. Peggy at once surmised that Billy was in some way responsible for the unrest.

"Perhaps my bugle call was a little theatrical," she began; "nevertheless it was the call to service of our new order of 'Camp Fire Minute Girls.'"

Mrs. Burton nodded. "Yes, I remember. The 'Camp Fire Minute Girls' are to pledge themselves to help in winning the war by food conservation, by praying for the triumph of the right, and by economizing in every possible way. I received a little booklet containing our new pledge and meant to speak of it to you."

In spite of the fact that Mrs. Burton was talking, she was not actually interested in what she was saying at the moment. Somewhere in the last row of her knitting she had dropped a stitch and while she spoke she was endeavoring to find it. As head of their small Red Cross society, Mrs. Webster was determined that their work should come up to the required standard. Knitting was not a natural art with Mrs. Burton and she particularly disliked unraveling her work after she supposed it finished.

Peggy reached over and quietly removed the gray sweater from her aunt's hands.

"You cannot pay attention to what anyone is saying and knit at the same time, Tante; I have seen you make the attempt before," Peggy remarked persuasively, "so please cease your efforts for a moment, as we have something of the utmost importance to talk about. Bettina, now that I have prepared the way, suppose you make things clearer. I have not your gift of words."

"It is only that we have been talking of the 'Camp Fire Minute Girls' and consider that we should follow the pledge very earnestly this summer," Bettina began. "We feel that really we ought to organize our camp fire on a new war basis. You have always been so generous to us, but this summer we wish to use only the new war recipes and to save and serve in every possible way. The advantage will be not only for the present time, but perhaps later with our own families. Peggy and I thought that we might even start a little garden near our camp, as vegetables grow so quickly in California. I suppose our ideas of helpfulness are rather vague and foolish, but that is why we wished to talk the situation over with you and Mrs. Webster and arrange some definite plan."

Mrs. Burton nodded. "An excellent idea, Bettina, and the sooner we Americans learn some method of less extravagant living the nearer we are to victory and the ending of the war. I wish I were a more apt pupil myself. Of course I am willing to agree with whatever you girls think best."

"Then we may help the soldiers in any way we like?" Sally Ashton inquired with such unexpected enthusiasm that everybody laughed.

"I do not care for any too strikingly original ideas of first-aid service, Sally," Mrs. Burton remonstrated.

Billy roused himself from his recumbent position and leaned forward. A single flame which had shot up from the smouldering fire cast a glow over his colorless face.

"I have been traveling with the Camp Fire party now for a good many weeks," he remarked in the suspiciously gentle manner with which he often began his verbal attacks, "and I am yet to hear one single word about an immediate peace. I cannot see what difference it will make in the end which country is victor. What the whole world must attain to is justice for every human being. I thought women were supposed to be the natural peace makers." Billy smiled — a malicious little smile which was vaguely irritating. "Women never have been peace makers or peace lovers. If they had do you suppose men would have continued fighting one another forever?"

"But, Billy —" Mrs. Burton began and suddenly ceased. A glance at her sister's face had been sufficient.

Besides, Dan Webster, released from his attention to Sally, had walked over and stood facing his mother and brother.

The two brothers, though, twins, were utterly unlike in appearance. For one thing, Dan was nearly six feet tall and splendidly built, with a vivid color and a suggestion of unusual physical health and power.

"I am sorry, Mother," he said in the voice he kept especially for his mother, "but I can't stay here and listen to Billy's nonsense and disloyalty. He is simply in love with the sound of his own voice and always has been. He has not the faintest understanding of the big things he talks about. I have stood a good deal from Billy first and last from the time we were children, because he was little and delicate and I was not supposed to treat him as I would have treated other fellows. I tell you candidly what Billy needs right now and what he always has needed is to have his head punched. He always has taken refuge in his delicacy and hidden behind women. He is doing the same thing now with all this peace talk and half-baked socialism. I wonder how far socialism would have traveled if men had never fought for their rights and the rights of other people? I wish the socialists in this country would think of that little fact now and then. I suppose if no one had ever fought for liberty, most of us would be slaves. But I seem to be talking as much as Billy! It is only this, Mother, don't you see that Billy and I cannot both remain with the Camp Fire party this summer? I don't wish it to happen, but I am afraid if he goes on as he has been doing—and you know nothing ever stops him—why, there will be trouble between us, that is all. If you will only give your consent I am sure I can persuade father to allow me to volunteer."

Mrs. Webster's eyes filled with tears. Dan was too interested in watching his mother to pay any attention to Billy's good-natured drawl.

"Good old Dan, there is some truth in what you say, I suppose. There is a little truth in most people's opinions. But what a story-book hero you will make some day! It is all right, your rubbing it in about my not being as strong as other fellows; I suppose you don't know that hurts a little."

"My dear Dan, I did not dream you could be so unreasonable!" Mrs. Webster returned, having finally gained sufficient control of her voice to speak. "You know perfectly well I shall never give my consent to your volunteering for any branch of the army until you have reached the draft age. Moreover, if you have a difficulty with Billy you know how much sorrow that means for me. Besides, your aunt and the girls and I need you here with us at our camp fire this summer. If I could, I would send Billy back to the farm instead of you, but he still needs the benefit of this southern climate."

Poor Mrs. Webster, like many other mothers, often found her children too great a problem for her solving.

By this time Billy was again prostrate on the earth with his eyes fixed upon the sky and apparently perfectly serene. Even his mother's statement in regard to sending him home had not disturbed him, although he and his father chronically misunderstood each other.

Dan was repentant. "Sorry, Mother," he said; "this was not the time or place for me to open this discussion with you. I am sure I beg everybody's pardon."

Then he turned and walked away.

CHAPTER IV

THE CAMP AND TEMPERAMENTAL EXCURSIONS

This summer in California for the first time the Sunrise camp was located near the sea.

After several days of investigating the countryside, in the meanwhile using the little mission town of Capistrano as their headquarters, the travelers discovered what they considered the ideal situation further south along the coast.

Near the border of one of the immense ranches for which southern California is famous they came upon a little stream of water flowing inside a channel. The channel had been deepened in order that the supply might last through the dry season. Not far away stood a small frame house. In harvest times the laborers on the ranch occupied this small house as a lodging for the night when the distance made it impossible for them to return to their own homes.

By a piece of rare good fortune Mrs. Burton was able for almost a nominal sum to rent this little place for her sister and herself.

The shack was lightly built, the roof formed of dried palm branches laid the one upon the other until the effect was like a thatched roof, although neither so warm nor so secure. Since it never rains during the summer in southern California, one requires only protection from the sun and wind. Near the house the camp-fire tents were set up in the form of a crescent.

Behind them the ranch stretched on for miles, a thousand-acre carpet of small green plants. For, as Marta Clark remarked when they were traveling down the state, it appeared as if California were preparing to provide the world with one gigantic bean feast.

Several hundreds of yards away the beach was silver and purple and rose with the sea verbena and ice plants which spread like a colorful embroidery over the sands. Here and there were tiny coves and clumps of rocks.

Near the camping site there was no main traveled road, but a small branch one which would improve with use. The closest place of human habitation was a seaside colony of artists, perhaps a mile or more beyond.

Here Mrs. Burton was able to find a garage for her automobile.

Partly because she was actually in need of his services and more to impress him with the idea, Mrs. Burton had persuaded Dan Webster to take charge of her car during the summer. As a matter of fact, aside from Billy, who did not always count, Dan was the only masculine person at the Sunrise camp, Mr. Jefferson Simpson having departed as casually as he originally had arrived, soon after the tents were set up.

Mrs. Burton preferred being shut away from strangers during their holidays and presumed the girls shared her desire.

Soon after their conversation about the camp fire a new régimé of war economy was established at Sunrise camp. There were uncomfortable moments when strange dishes of none too appetizing a character were produced. But always the cooks declared it the fault of the too particular persons who refused to partake of them and not of the food itself. They did acquire new methods of bread making, substituting bran and corn-meal for wheat flour which were really improvements on the old. Moreover, the summer before the Indian girl, Dawapa, had taught the Sunrise Camp Fire members a number of the old Indian uses of corn. With perishable fruits and vegetables so abundant, it was unnecessary, during the summer at least, to suffer any real discomfort from war economies.

Now and then one of the girls would develop a too rigorous idea of self-denial to meet with the approval of her Camp Fire guardian. But after a time Mrs. Burton ceased to worry over original departures, permitting the girls to adjust matters for themselves.

However, it is not the adjustment of mere material things which is the difficult problem with human beings in living together, but the adjustment of one unlike nature with another.

As much as possible after his open disagreement with Billy, Dan Webster endeavored to avoid his brother's society. They never had been congenial or spent much time together since the days when they were children. But at present Dan and Billy were sleeping in the same tent at night and in the daytime Billy was always mooning about camp insisting upon one of the girls listening to him. He preferred Vera, but if she were too busy, any one of the other girls could substitute.

This would have made no difference to Dan except that Billy blandly and serenely continued to expound his views upon peace in spite of the fact that every member of Sunrise camp disagreed with him.

Hard as it was to endure, Dan's hands were tied, for he had solemnly promised his mother not to use physical violence with Billy, and nothing else would stop the flow of his misplaced eloquence.

So, as Dan was an ardent fisherman, he used to spend days away from camp fishing and swimming. He was fond of the Camp Fire girls, especially of Marta Clark and of Sally Ashton, but he could not endure too large a diet of exclusively feminine society. Moreover, Dan was too accomplished an athlete and too fine a fellow all round not to make friends wherever he went among men.

One afternoon it chanced that Dan was alone and preparing to go in swimming at a rather dangerous point about three miles below Sunrise camp.

The spot was deserted and Dan was beginning to undress when he became conscious of the uncomfortable sensation that some one at no great distance off was watching him.

Glancing about, Dan discovered the calm figure of his brother standing only a few yards away when he had sincerely hoped that at least several miles separated them.

In reply to Billy's friendly "hello," his brother returned no answer. Nevertheless Billy strolled quietly across the space between them, taking a seat on the rocky cliff, apparently as cheerful and undisturbed as if he considered himself a welcome interruption.

"Better not go in swimming from this cliff, Dan; this place looks pretty unsafe. The waves are so violent you might be thrown against the rocks," he began, offering his entirely unsolicited advice in the most affable manner.

As a matter of fact, upon most occasions, Dan Webster was rather unusually sweet tempered. But at present, because of his own disappointment over not being allowed to volunteer for some branch of war service, and because of what he considered his brother's disloyal opinions, the very sight of Billy enraged him.

"Billy Webster, I wonder if you are a coward about every mortal thing? I suppose you understand that cowardice is what I believe lies at the back of your pacifism. I suppose it is natural to wish to call an ugly fact by a pretty name. Besides, it is a lot pleasanter and easier to talk about the beauty and sacredness of peace and the rights of men than to fight and die for them. But please don't trouble about me and run along back to camp. I don't want to go into this subject with you again as I came away largely to get rid of your society." Dan made an effort to speak quietly.

"All right, I'll be off in a moment; don't wish to worry you," Billy agreed, and, except for a slight flush which Dan did not observe, he appeared unmoved. "Do you know I am glad you reopened this subject. Ever since you spoke of the same thing the other day I have been wondering if what you said was true and I am a pacifist because I am a physical coward. Of course I know I am afraid of a lot of things that don't frighten you, but I believe you are mistaken about this business, Dan. If I were up against a stiff proposition I might still be afraid and yet go through with it. My feeling about peace really has nothing to do with the part I may some day be called upon to play in this war, a pretty poor part at best I expect. I wish you would believe this if you can. But good-by; I am off."

Then, before Dan could make any response, Billy moved away. Once out of sight, he lay down upon the beach with his head propped on his slender hands, keeping a watchful outlook upon Dan, who was swimming nearly a mile out from the shore. When Dan had finished and climbed back up the cliff, then only did Billy set out for Sunrise camp.

There were also temperamental difficulties, needing adjustment among the Camp Fire girls.

Frankly, both Sally Ashton and Gerry Williams had been bored by their long journey down the California coast and their many pilgrimages to the old Spanish missions along their route. With their natures it was impossible for either of them to understand how any human being could obtain a great deal of pleasure from mere scenery and what persons were pleased to call romantic atmosphere. To Sally and Gerry romance took shape in a very different guise.

During the trip they were at least sustained by the hope that, once settled in their summer camp, they would begin making agreeable acquaintances, notwithstanding, up to the present time, Sunrise camp had developed about as many social opportunities as a desert island.

Therefore, one morning, with the perfectly definite plan of going forth in search of adventure, Sally and Gerry set out upon a little temperamental excursion.

CHAPTER V

ABALONE SHELLS

After their summer holiday together at the Grand Canyon the Sunrise Camp Fire girls had been separated during the previous winter, returning to their own homes. Nevertheless, they kept in touch with one another and, as a matter of fact, among the seven girls only Gerry Williams' history had remained a mystery to the others.

From the moment of her appearance upon the west-bound train with Mrs. Burton, who had introduced her as the new member of their Camp Fire group, not a word had been spoken concerning Gerry's past. Mrs. Burton must have regarded her friendship as a sufficient guarantee, since ever afterwards she and Gerry had continued equally reticent, not even confiding under what circumstances they originally had learned to know each other.

Naturally such secrecy aroused a certain degree of curiosity, and now and then one of the Camp Fire girls would ask Gerry a question, thinking her answer must betray some small fact in her past. But either she would evade the question or else politely decline to answer.

She was poor — no one could continue blind to this actuality — but whether her parents were living or dead, whether she had any other relatives, no one could find out from Gerry herself or from her Camp Fire guardian.

In truth, Gerry made no effort to conceal how intensely disagreeable she considered a lack of money, freely announcing that poverty always had been the bane of her past existence and that she asked nothing more from the future than to be safely delivered from it.

Occasionally some one would whisperingly question whether Mrs. Burton would continue her bounty to Gerry when the Camp Fire holidays were over; yet no one had sufficiently bad taste to make this inquiry. Mrs. Webster knew no more than the others. She made no effort to keep up with her Sister Polly's many generosities, which were frequently as erratic as the lady herself. Only to her husband would Mrs. Burton confide the extent of her efforts to help other people. She preferred doing things in her own way.

One circumstance was freely discussed between Mrs. Burton and her protégé. During the past winter Gerry had developed a desire to study art and Mrs. Burton had arranged for her lessons. Yet Gerry made no pretense of having any especial talent or of being very deeply interested in her work. She was also frank in stating that she did not care a great deal for the outdoor camping life, aside from the fact that Mrs. Burton considered the influence of living with the other Camp Fire girls of value to her. The great attraction in the experience for Gerry, as she freely stated, was the opportunity it offered to be near her famous friend.

Nevertheless, after a winter's study at the Art Institute in Chicago, Gerry had learned to make pretty outdoor studies of flowers and other small objects. She had a good deal of feeling for color and design, which she declared due to her interest in clothes. Her Camp Fire guardian encouraged her attention to art as much as possible, often excusing Gerry from everyday tasks, that she might give more time to her sketching.

Just why she should be thus favored the other Camp Fire girls did not understand, yet Gerry appreciated the reason.

Also less was always expected of her, and her weaknesses were more readily forgiven. The one foolish act of revenge upon Bettina had caused the only serious difficulty with her Camp Fire guardian, and apparently even this had been forgotten.

On the morning of their excursion Gerry had announced that she wished to spend the day sketching along the coast and that Sally had been kind enough to agree to accompany her.

The greater part of the time the two girls were extremely intimate and if now and then a slight coolness arose between them it never continued long, as they had too many common bonds of interest.

Both girls were charmingly pretty and an entire contrast. Sally Ashton's eyes and hair were brown, her lips full with an up-ward curve and her skin, which the sun and wind never seemed to tan, as soft and white as a baby's. She was small and plump and her figure had no angles.

One might have been deluded by Sally's yielding and feminine appearance into the impression that she could be easily influenced by stronger natures than her own. The fact is that Sally was never really influenced except when she chose to be.

Realizing this, Mrs. Burton made no effort to interrupt her friendship with Gerry Williams, which was just as well since nothing is more difficult than to interfere with a friendship between two girls who feel a mutual attraction and see each other frequently.

Gerry Williams' prettiness was of a more unusual character. She had the delicate fairness which one so rarely sees in its perfection. Her hair was a pale gold, yet the gold was undeniably there. Her eyes were light blue and held the clearness, the indelible, transparent blueness of certain pieces of rare old china. Her small head was set upon a rather long fair throat and as she walked with a peculiar lightness and grace it was almost as if she might at any moment break into dancing steps. About Gerry's nature there were elements which were frankly commonplace, nevertheless her appearance suggested one of the dancing figures upon an ancient Greek frieze.

This morning she and Sally wore their everyday Camp Fire costumes, and because it was cool their Navajo sweater coats, Gerry's a bright scarlet and Sally's an Oxford blue. They intended being away all day, and besides Gerry's sketching outfit they carried their luncheon.

The girls had chosen to go in the direction of the artists' colony only a few miles away. Over both the water and land there was the haze of the early hours at the seaside, and yet the mist was only a light one and more agreeable than the hot sun which would come later in the day.

The land was gay with flowers. On the hillside there were tall bunches of cacti, one variety bearing a bright yellow flower like a silken poppy. The ordinary jimson weed grew so large that each blossom looked like a great white lily.

On the side toward the beach the tiny beads of water glistening amid the rose color of the ice plants shone like tiny fairy jewels.

Past the groups of houses which presumably sheltered famous artists as well as amateurs, perhaps with no more ability than Gerry, the two girls wandered on, absorbed in their own conversation.

They were not especially disappointed at finding no one in the neighborhood of the colony who seemed to be of interest. There were three or four girls idling in one of the yards who stared curiously as the Camp Fire girls passed, but Sally and Gerry paid but slight attention to them in return, having previously confessed to each other that they were a little tired of so much feminine society.

A tall old gentleman with a white, closely trimmed beard strode by, carrying a large canvas under his arm. He frowned portentously, as if he would have the girls appreciate that he was a genius in the grasp of a creative impulse and so must not be disturbed. Neither Sally nor Gerry had the faintest impulse toward disturbing him, yet his appearance suggested a train of thought to Sally.

"I wonder, Gerry, why you decided so suddenly that you wished to study art?" she said. "Until this summer I have never even heard you mention the subject. Do you intend making a business of it some day? You won't mind my speaking of this, but you have always said you had to do something or other to make your own living."

Instead of replying at once Gerry hummed the first line of a song, also moving on so quickly that Sally, who was averse to violent exercise, had difficulty in keeping up with her.

"Certainly not, Sally," she answered finally. "Besides, if I ever should develop such a foolish idea, who do you think would buy my silly little pictures, except perhaps Mrs. Burton? I do wish she were my real aunt; I am oftentimes jealous of Peggy. But really I began studying art last winter chiefly on her account. She insisted that I should not idle away all my time, so I concluded that I would prefer being an art student to attending a regular school.

"Mrs. Burton was delighted, because she thinks it would be a good plan for me to become a dressmaker or a designer. I am so fond of clothes and she believes the art lessons will be of value to my future work. However, my dear Sally, nothing is further from my own expectations. You and I for different reasons must make marriage our career. You were created for domesticity and I, well, I simply must marry some one with money. I used to hope that Mrs. Burton might do a great deal for me some day, before I knew about her own family and her Camp Fire group. Now I realize that she only intends helping me to help myself, as the highly moral phrase goes."

"But haven't you any people of your own, or any close friends?" Sally demanded with the persistency which belonged to her disposition. Half a dozen times before she had asked this same question without receiving a satisfactory reply.

Gerry only laughed good naturedly. Sally's curiosity amused her.

"No people and no friends I care to talk about, my dear. You know I have told you this several times before."

In spite of the fact that by this time the girls had walked for three or four miles, up until now Gerry had not suggested sitting down to begin her sketching. At this moment she moved over to the edge of a cliff, glancing down at the beach below.

"Come, Sally, see what a fascinating place I have discovered. Suppose we climb down to the beach; you must be tired and I may be able to work for a little while. I do want to have something to show Mrs. Burton as a result of our day."

On the beach the girls saw a little wooden hut with a huge kettle filled with boiling water standing before the door. Half a mile or more out in the ocean two Japanese fishermen were diving for the famous abalone shells, while on the sands a dozen of the shells, having been thoroughly cleansed, now lay drying in the sun; their inner surfaces of mother-of-pearl held all the colors of the dawn.

CHAPTER VI

"MY OWN WILL COME TO ME"

Whether consciously or unconsciously, the thing we most desire in this world will come to us in the end.

Rather precipitately Sally and Gerry climbed down the side of the cliff to the beach. The way was steep and now and then Sally had to be encouraged and assisted until both girls finally arrived on the sands a little out of breath.

The beach stretched on further than one could see, a pale golden carpet now that the mists were clearing. It was divided at this point by a narrow gully. On one side of the gully were uneven platforms of rocks and between these rocks ran little streams of salt water from the ocean, creating tiny tidal lakes and rivulets.

Up and down these rocks, sometimes disappearing inside the water, at others clinging perilously above its edge, or hiding behind sprays of sea lichen or fern, were innumerable small sea monsters. At times the sides of the rocks were alive with hundreds, even thousands, of tiny crabs; then one single unexpected noise and off they scuttled like an army, not in dignified retreat but in utter rout.

The girls having descended the cliff, rested for a few moments and then wandered along these ledges. They were not of a dangerous character, for most of the stones were flat and not too far apart to be safely crossed.

Yet they walked slowly. Occasionally they stopped to watch two fishermen at work. The men were Japanese divers, and it was fascinating to see them swim with quiet, even strokes out into the deep water and then dive down heads first to remain under a terrifying length of time. Yet as each man rose again usually he had secured one or more of the large abalone shells.

In spite of their interest, Sally Ashton pleaded that they remain at a safe distance from the two men. As a matter of fact, Sally frequently suffered from the small timidities which belonged to her particular type of intensely feminine character. Although not in the least timid herself, Gerry agreed, it being a wise custom of hers to give way to her companion in unimportant matters. Moreover, she really intended working seriously for a few hours. Now that she and Sally were both weary, this sheltered place along the beach would be as suitable as any other to begin her painting.

Finding a comfortable surface of clean sand on a broad ledge of rock, with other rocks in the background, Gerry sat down. Here there was less wind than in other places and sufficient room for Sally to lie close beside her.

At about the correct distance away, a small boat moored to some hidden anchor moved back and forth with the movement of the waves.

This boat appeared a suitable subject to Gerry for her sketch. She had no idea of making a success of so ambitious a subject, but since all that Mrs. Burton asked of her was industry and not high artistry, Gerry was willing to work now and then. She really did wish to please her Camp Fire guardian, and if her motives were a little mixed and not all of them of the noblest character, well, there are others of us in this world who have mixed motives beside Gerry Williams!

After the first few moments of settling down to her task, Gerry began to feel mildly interested in her effort.

Her surroundings were in themselves an inspiration.

Nearby, and using her friend's crimson sweater as a pillow, Sally Ashton had curled herself up in the sunshine. She was wearing her own blue one for warmth. There was but little breeze stirring and the sun had grown suddenly hot, but Sally had a passionate affection for warmth. She had also an endless capacity for sleeping when there was nothing of interest in life to make wakefulness worth while.

For a few moments she watched Gerry at work, thinking she had never seen her look so pretty or labor so industriously. Then Sally viewed the small boat whose continuous movement impressed her like the sleepy swaying of a cradle. Afterwards she fell into a state of semi-conscious dreaming.

But Gerry kept on with her sketching certainly for more than an hour. By the end of that time she was surprised to find what a lovely sketch she had made. In spite of the fact that her boat was out of drawing, the color in her sky line was beautiful and the waves of the sea suggested real water and a real ocean.

After gazing at her painting with wholly unexpected admiration, Gerry put it carefully away in her sketch book. She was feeling a little tired, but her act was inspired more by discretion than weariness. To work upon her sketch any longer would probably destroy the value it at present possessed and Mrs. Burton would be pleased by her success.

Believing Sally to be fast asleep and not wishing to disturb her for a time, Gerry, leaning forward and resting her chin on her two folded hands, fell to dreaming.

For the past ten days or more, ever since her arrival in southern California, it seemed to Gerry Williams that never had her dreams and her desires been so insistent. She did not know that this was the influence of the semi-tropical climate upon her physical and spiritual development.

In truth, Gerry's past life had been a trying one and there was no reason why she should have been content with it, or why she should not hope for a happier future.

These summers in Arcady with Mrs. Burton—for they had been as summers in Arcady to the Sunrise Hill Camp Fire girls—had been the fairest experiences in Gerry's history. Yet she professed no ardent love for the outdoors as the other girls did. Neither was she so young as some of them, since within a few weeks she would be eighteen.

There would be other summers to come, Gerry realized, when she would not be Mrs. Burton's guest. Indeed, the Camp Fire guardian had frankly stated that if the war continued they would not be able to have their holidays together. In the future she must devote her money, her time and her energy to war service.

So today, looking out over the water, but now that her sketching was over, no longer interested in the view, Gerry faced what seemed to her an interminable number of lonely summers and winters and springs and autumns. In her earlier acquaintance with Mrs. Burton, when the great lady had revealed an unexpected interest in her, Gerry, as she had lately confessed to Sally Ashton, had dreamed impossible dreams. In those days she had imagined herself as Mrs. Burton's ward, living in her home, or traveling about with her over the world meeting rich and famous people.

Then at the last Gerry's vision had always been a wealthy marriage. A foolish dream perhaps, and yet not original or uncommon!

She did not think of her marriage as bringing her love or spiritual happiness, only wealth and social prominence. But at this time in her life Gerry of course believed that the last two possessions represented the character of happiness she sought.

Having awakened to reality with regard to Mrs. Burton's attitude, appreciating that she felt for her only a kindly interest and a moderate affection, Gerry was the more intent upon discovering some immediate solution for her own future.

From this summer in California she had hoped a great deal. She had thought through Mrs. Burton's prominence that it might be possible to make wealthy and worth-while friends. Now it appeared that the Camp Fire guardian intended to have her group of girls spend a secluded summer, deriving their entertainment from their life together outdoors in this beautiful place.

In consequence Gerry was deeply disappointed. Today she felt that the prospect ahead was dreary and dissatisfying. Mrs. Burton expected her to work and had no notion of assisting her toward any other fate. She had made her own way in the world and believed that work brought one the finest satisfaction. But Gerry recognized her own commonplaceness and understood that unconsciously Mrs. Burton was not altogether fair. Of course, if one possessed great talent, then work lifted you above dullness and routine, brought you beauty and joy. Yet she could only picture herself pursuing some stupid task, since she had neither education nor especial ability in any direction. Her only gifts, prettiness and her desire for the refinements of life which always had been denied her, little in truth to offer when there was no one to help!

Then, intending to banish her attack of blues, Gerry jumped up hurriedly. As she did so she noticed the two Japanese divers. They had left their work and had come softly over the sands until at the present moment they were only a few feet off. They were talking in excited voices, holding up the deep-bowled abalone shells, now polished and shining, and evidently trying to attract attention.

For an instant Gerry was puzzled. Then, before she could speak or even stir again, Sally, startled from sleep, also leaped to her feet. She may have been frightened by Gerry's sudden movement and now, catching sight of the Japanese fishermen, may have been under the impression that they had frightened Gerry. Whatever the cause, with an exclamation of terror, she started running, uttering funny little cries of alarm.

First Gerry merely called out reassuringly, then, perceiving that Sally would not stop, she ran after her.

Sally was awkward; she kept stumbling and sliding over the ledges of rock, making no effort to be sure of her foothold or to choose the easiest way. In the beginning Gerry was amused, then she grew a little nervous. Sally was always the least athletic of the Camp Fire girls.

"Do be careful; the men are only trying to sell us their shells. They have no idea of frightening you," Gerry expostulated.

She expected to reach Sally in time to keep her from injuring herself. But suddenly Sally gave an exclamation both of fright and pain; having made a false estimate of the space between two ledges of rock, she found herself falling into a small ravine.

The ravine was not deep; nevertheless Sally's rescue was not simple, since she would not help herself. Finally Gerry had to summon to her assistance the two Japanese, who had innocently caused the catastrophe. At last a bruised and tearful Sally was deposited upon a comfortable resting place. But here Sally declared she must remain indefinitely, as she was "far too seriously hurt ever to walk again."

The situation was trying, and Gerry was at her wits' end till one small inspiration came to her. Since food had ever a reviving effect upon Sally, they could have their luncheon and perhaps afterwards she would feel stronger.

But although her appetite remained unaffected by her accident, the afternoon wore on with Sally still insisting that she could not stir one step. Moreover, any suggestion of Gerry's leaving to find help always reduced her to tears.

Yet something must be done!

Long ago the little Japanese fishermen had returned to their tasks. Sitting cross-legged on the sand at some distance off, Gerry could see them patiently at work cleaning and polishing their shells. She remembered that they had seemed to understand what she had said, although speaking only a few English words.

Walking over to them Gerry as simply as possible presented their predicament.

When she had finished speaking the small bright-eyed men glanced at each other and nodded.

"Alle-ight," one of them answered for both.

Then off they trotted, this time disappearing inside their small hut. Next moment they returned carrying on their shoulders a flat straw basket set upon two long poles. It was scarcely a basket, so much as a woven straw mat, which the divers probably used at odd times for transporting their sea merchandise.

Ultimately Sally was persuaded to allow herself to be hoisted upon this mat, which was fairly strong since it suffered her weight. Then the two little men bore her off, swinging easily between them. They ran lightly from rock to rock until climbing up the cliff they reached the road at the summit, with Gerry following as swiftly as possible.

They had arranged not to attempt to carry Sally to camp but to some place nearer at hand, where she could receive aid.

Originally when they had made this plan it appeared to Gerry as a reasonable one and not one to cause anxiety. Now as she pursued the two strange little men, who were carrying Sally with such ease and quickness to a perfectly unknown destination she had a curious sensation more of bewilderment than fear.

However, one had to keep moving so rapidly that there was small opportunity for clear thinking.

Leaving the main road, the little men struck into another, which went first up a bare brown hill and then down again. The second hill was green with a crop of the ever-present beans.

Finally they climbed to the top of a mesa and brought Sally to a resting place before a clump of dusty, gray-green pepper trees.

On their left was a hedge of untrimmed shrubs and in front an open court. Beyond stood an old Spanish ranch house.

After whispering together, one of the little men rang a bell, which hung on a stand outside this court.

A few moments later a Japanese servant appeared and the three men spoke to one another in Japanese. Then the servant turned away.

It was all very unusual and puzzling. Before Sally and Gerry could be overwhelmed by uneasiness, to their relief they observed an older man and two young men approaching. They were obviously gentlemen, and one of them Gerry thought the most attractive fellow she had ever seen in her life. Yet he did not look like an American, but what her imagination had pictured as a Spaniard. He must have been about twenty-two or three and possessed unusually dark hair and eyes and skin.

When Gerry had explained their difficulty and apologized for their intrusion, their host led the way through the outer court into the enclosed one.

Sally continued to be borne aloft like a foreign princess upon the shoulders of her faithful Caryatids.

The inside court was a miniature fairyland.

Like all really old Spanish ranch houses, this house was built in the form of a square with the garden in the center. It was of one story with the veranda also on the inside and running the entire length of the house.

In days long past this veranda would have been filled with people, for when the Spanish ranch houses were the center of California's social life all the play and work of the Spanish families, their friends and servants took place outdoors.

Now the two Camp Fire girls saw no one save their hosts and the one man servant; there was no faintest suggestion of the presence of a woman.

The place looked old and ramshackle, as if its owners had preferred to enjoy life rather than to improve their estate. Even the enclosed garden, notwithstanding it was a sheer glory of flowers, showed neglect. A bougainvillea vine had been allowed to grow so large that it covered one-third of the veranda, hanging like a flowery canopy above one portion of the garden. Along the paths oleanders were set out in unpainted wooden tubs and the rose bushes had gone so long untrimmed that they were now of great size and covered with tiny white and yellow flowers.

Once this garden had been carefully planned and cared for, yet, perhaps, at present it held an even deeper charm.

Naturally, soon after their arrival their host, Mr. Philip Morris, had introduced himself and his younger companions, and Gerry Williams had given her own and Sally's name. Gerry also had explained the circumstances of Sally's accident and the fact that they were members of a camping party who were spending the summer on the California coast.

The young man who had originally attracted her attention proved to be the son of Mr. Morris. In introducing him the father accorded the Spanish pronunciation to his name, "Felipe," which he had not used with his own.

Later it developed that Felipe's mother had been Spanish and the old ranch the property of her family from the days when California was a province of Spain. But as she was dead it was true that at present no woman was a member of their household.

The other young fellow, Merton Anderson, was the son of a neighbor and a guest. As he had ridden over to the Morris ranch on horseback he offered to take back any message Sally and Gerry might care to send their friends, for Mr. Morris insisted that Sally must not be moved again until she had seen a physician.

At last Gerry wrote a note to Mrs. Burton explaining what had occurred and asking advice. If it were possible would she not drive over to the ranch in her automobile and bear Sally safely back to camp?

CHAPTER VII

THE SACRIFICE OF YOUTH

About ten o'clock on the evening of the same day Mrs. Burton and Mr. Morris were sitting before the open door of the old Spanish house looking out over the countryside.

In the neighborhood of the California coast the moonlight has a rare brilliancy. The mists of the early morning and late afternoons usually disappear and seem to float overhead in white and silver clouds.

"You are very kind to allow us to impose upon your hospitality in this fashion, Mr. Morris," Mrs. Burton declared, in the voice whose rare quality gave even to her ordinary statements a charm beyond other persons. "I don't believe I have ever seen so beautiful a view in California as I am having from your house tonight, and yet a few hours ago I would not have believed this possible."

Immediately upon receipt of Gerry Williams' note Mrs. Burton had motored over to the Morris ranch, using Merton Anderson as her guide. She was anxious, of course, in regard to Sally's injuries, but anxious also to learn the character of her rescuers. Naturally the girls could not be allowed to remain alone over night with strangers. Unless Sally were in a really critical condition, she could certainly be moved without danger.

Within a few minutes after Mrs. Burton's arrival at the ranch, the physician who had been telephoned for some time before, appeared in answer to the summons.

After seeing Sally he announced that she was not seriously hurt, only bruised and shaken, and could be moved without difficulty. Despite this assurance, the two girls and Mrs. Burton were spending the night at the ranch.

"I don't believe you appreciate, Mrs. Burton, how great a pleasure and an honor your presence in our home is both to my son and me. We are so far out of the world and with no women in our family are often extremely lonely. However, we are not so remote that we have not heard of Mrs. Burton's distinguished reputation."

Mr. Morris spoke with an old-fashioned courtesy and admiration which no one could fail to appreciate.

His guest preferred not to talk of her professional life during her summer holidays with the Camp Fire girls.

"At least I am sure we shall never forget our own pleasure," Mrs. Burton returned. "The fact of the matter was I discovered at once that Sally and Gerry were determined upon remaining as soon as you and your son were kind enough to invite us. It is my private belief that Sally even pretended to be more seriously hurt in order to influence my decision. She appears to be enjoying the rôle of injured heroine, and yet I can scarcely criticise the girls, as I did not require a great deal of persuasion."

As a matter of fact, soon after her arrival she also had fallen a victim to the beauty and romantic aspect of the old Spanish estate and to the charm and hospitality of its owners. Moreover, Mrs. Burton realized that Mr. Morris and his son were sincerely desirous of having them as guests. Their invitation had not been merely a conventional one and the old house seemed to possess an almost indefinite number of shabby bedrooms.

With an expressive gesture of her hands Mrs. Burton suddenly arose and walked with her host to the edge of the hill which sloped down from the front of his house.

"You are not very far out of the world when, as you tell me, the new National Guard camp is being built on the broad mesa below you. Is it where I see the little row of lights? Wherever our soldiers are is the only world that is of much importance these days! I am to drive over soon and see the new cantonment. My Camp Fire girls and I are anxious to find out if we can be of the least possible service. Recently, for the first time in my life, there have been moments when I was sorry to be a woman."

"And yet it is a sadder thing to be an old man, Mrs. Burton. I offered my services at the beginning, but I am past sixty and — well — well, they were right, of course; I am not a trained soldier and not even a competent business man and I should only have been a nuisance."

In the impetuous fashion which had always been characteristic of her girlhood as Polly O'Neill and which she had never lost, Mrs. Burton turned around.

"Yes, it is hard. Women are not soldiers at heart, in spite of those thrilling Russian women and their great 'Battalion of Death.' We are not intended for the actual fighting and can only do our work behind the lines until the world is purified forever from the scourge of war. But you have your son to take your place."

For a few moments Mr. Morris made no reply. Then he replied slowly in a tone of hesitation and of embarrassment:

"I wonder if you will allow me to make a confidant of you? I am in great trouble, Mrs. Burton, and although we were strangers before this evening I know your life must have taught you to understand human nature. My son does not wish to enter the war. I tried to persuade him to volunteer. He refused. Now the draft has come and his number has been called, he is still making every effort to escape military service, pleading exemption upon entirely unnecessary grounds. The fact is inexplicable to me. When my son was born my wife and I were no longer young and she died a short time after. Felipe has grown up here with me, with his friends and his flowers and his music, to which he is sincerely devoted, and nothing has ever been required of him. I knew he was indolent and selfish perhaps, but until the United States entered the war I failed to appreciate that Felipe was not a man. Another circumstance which has added to our difficulty, instead of clearing it away, is that Felipe and I have recently inherited a large sum of money. Until recently, as our home must have revealed to you, we have been poor and not very industrious. Now our inheritance has made my son more than ever eager for a life of ease and pleasure. He has been planning to fix up the old place until it looks as it did many years ago. He wishes also to study singing, as he has a really beautiful voice, and has been talking of going to Spain, now that the other European countries are at present out of the question. You can see I scarcely know what to do. Felipe's exemption claim is almost sure to be denied, and yet I cannot discuss the matter with our friends and neighbors. I do not wish to prejudice them against my boy. What is it I can do, Mrs. Burton, when I confess to you that I appear to have no influence with my son upon the subject of his responsibility to his country?"

Mrs. Burton continued looking down upon the extraordinary view.

The hills toward the east were black and eerie, the sea to the west a shining mirror, with the valleys like shadows in between.

"Mr. Morris, I wish you and your son would come over to our camp some day soon," she remarked later with apparent irrelevance. "Of course I wish you to know my sister, but I should also like you to meet her sons. One of them, Dan Webster, is one of the finest type of American boys. He is strong and clean and good looking and has no dearer wish in life than to be allowed to volunteer. In another year I presume my sister will be forced to give her consent—Dan is only seventeen at present. My other nephew, Billy—well, I hardly know how to describe Billy, because he is like no other human being I have ever known. He is one of the most impossible and obstinate boys in the world, and one never knows from one moment to the next what he is going to do or say. At present he is the trial of all our lives at Sunrise camp; he has proclaimed himself a pacifist, and feels called upon to convert everybody he meets. He is filled with Tolstoi's beautiful theories of universal peace. As he is still too young for the draft his ideas so far have not proved a serious menace, and yet I worry over him a good deal. Nevertheless, do you know I am not sure Billy would not be as heroic as Dan if the test ever comes and he is once convinced peace can only follow the tragic sacrifice of war.

45

"I am not saying all this to you, Mr. Morris, because I am unsympathetic about your son. It is perhaps because I believe I may understand his attitude. Forgive me if you do not agree with me, but I wonder if we older people are fully appreciating what tremendous sacrifices this war is demanding of youth. We have no right to expect all of them to give up their individual hopes and dreams for the future without hesitating and without flinching. They cannot all be made of the blood of heroes. The amazing fact is that so many of them have been. Personally I cannot help being a little sorry for your son. He will do the right thing in time, I am sure, but it cannot be easy to surrender this exquisite home and his ambition for a musical life. Felipe is probably afflicted with the artistic temperament, or else inspired by it, and the ways of the artistic temperament are past finding out," Mrs. Burton concluded, endeavoring to add a somewhat lighter tone to the conversation.

Her host shook his head gravely.

"You are very kind, Madame, and yet I am afraid I cannot accept your defense of my son. His ancestors were Spanish adventurers and soldiers and my own fought with Washington. However, I shall be delighted to visit your camp. One of the many reasons I wished to persuade you to remain over night with us was in order that Felipe might learn to know the girls who are with you. I fancied that he was immediately interested in one of them. Perhaps later she may prove an inspiration, a spur to him. American girls must have no patience with slackers these days. But suppose we cease talking about the war which haunts us all so everlastingly. Won't you walk with me and look at some of the other views about the old place by moonlight?"

Mrs. Burton and her host entered the front door of the house, crossed the large sitting room and came out upon one of the paths of the enclosed garden.

Now the air was almost suffocatingly sweet with the night fragrances of the semi-tropical flowers.

Under the deep magenta canopy of the bougainvillea vine the older woman discovered Gerry and her younger host.

Felipe Morris was holding a guitar, but for the moment he and Gerry were quietly talking. Feeling too shaken and uncomfortable to remain out of bed, and realizing by feminine intuition that Felipe would prefer to be alone with Gerry, Sally Ashton had retired some time before.

Now, although Mrs. Burton made no effort to interrupt Gerry's whispered conversation with Felipe Morris, she did wonder a little curiously what her influence upon the young man would be, if by chance he had been attracted by her.

There was no denying Gerry's exquisite prettiness; tonight with her pale gold hair, her fairness and grace she seemed in tune with the beauty of this old-world garden. Yet Mrs. Burton believed that Gerry was shallow and vain and that her ideas of life included less of devotion to duty and self-sacrifice than Felipe's. It was difficult to conceive of her acting as a motive force to high endeavor, Gerry, who dreamed only of money and pretty clothes and what she was pleased to consider "society."

Then Mrs. Burton sighed as she followed her host into the land which lay on the other side of the hedge. Had one the right to demand that Gerry and Felipe think of war tonight in a shrine, dedicated like this enclosed garden, to the service of youth and romance?

CHAPTER VIII

FELIPE

As soon as Mrs. Burton and his father were out of sight Felipe began singing:

"I will make you brooches and toys for your delightOf bird-song at morning and star-shine at night.I will make a palace fit for you and me,Of green days in forests and blue days at sea.

"I will make my kitchen and you shall keep your roomWhere white flows the river and bright blows the broomAnd you shall wash your linen and keep your body whiteIn rainfall at morning and dewfall at night.

"And this shall be for music when no one else is near,The fine song for singing, the rare song to hear!That only I remember, that only you admire,On the broad road that stretches and the roadside fire."

Then Felipe's song ended, and yet it seemed to Gerry that she could still hear the inflections of his voice.

"Thank you; that was lovely. I did not know I cared so much for music before," the girl answered simply and without the least touch of coquetry which one might have expected of a girl like Gerry in such surroundings. "But what an exquisite voice you have and what a beautiful night it is! I am sure I do not remember another half so lovely."

Then Gerry leaned forward a little so that she could see more clearly out into the garden.

"I don't wonder you feel that you cannot give all this up," she continued, with a graceful movement of her hand. "It seems to me wicked that you should be forced into the war, hating it as you do and perhaps spoiling your future as a singer. I agree with you, one ought to live his own life. All men are not equally fitted to be soldiers."

Gerry spoke with an unexpected vehemence which rather surprised her. For the past hour Felipe Morris had been pouring forth his side of the war problem to her, but as he was an entire stranger there was no especial reason why she should be so disturbed over the thought of his being forced to enter the army.

"I suppose I understand why you so hate giving up your home and your life here on the ranch and your music and all the rest, because I have never had a home of my own, or any possessions of much value," Gerry ended in a quieter voice and manner.

"You possess nothing of value!" Felipe Morris repeated, and although he said nothing more Gerry felt oddly flattered and happy.

Then Felipe laughed unexpectedly.

"I wonder if you realize, Miss Williams, that we have seen each other before tonight, probably about ten days or more ago? My friend Merton Anderson and I chanced to be spending the night at San Juan Capistrano when you and your friends rode into the old mission town. You don't know how much curiosity your appearance excited. You gave the old town the greatest thrill it has had in a long time. You see the little town is more than half foreign; there are Spaniards and Mexicans and half-breed Indians. You were dressed in a kind of compromise Indian costume, and down there we had never seen or heard of the Camp Fire. Merton and I hid ourselves on one of the verandas and sang a duet for your benefit. Then later, when it was too dark for us to see one another distinctly, we followed your party about the mission grounds."

Gerry frowned and then blushed a little from embarrassment.

"Were you wearing Mexican costumes? I confess Sally and I did become interested in you, but we supposed of course that you were either Mexicans or Spaniards. Your song was in Spanish so that we could not understand it."

"Shall I sing to you in Spanish now?" Felipe returned. "I speak the language as readily as I do English. You see my mother was of Spanish origin and she and an old nurse who lives near here always spoke in Spanish to me when I was a kid. You were right about the Mexican costumes. Anderson and I had been over into Mexico for a few days and were on our way home. I like to escape over there now and then when life at the ranch becomes too slow. I can be mistaken for a Mexican when I wish and it is sometimes amusing."

Gerry nodded, preferring to have Felipe talk to her rather than to offer him confidences. Oddly she was wishing tonight that she had read as many books as the other Camp Fire girls and had enjoyed the same advantages.

"Then you saw all seven of us at Capistrano?" she asked at length; adding, "There are five other girls in our Camp Fire group."

Felipe laughed. "Yes, I saw all of you, yet it was you alone I remembered," he murmured with true Spanish gallantry.

"Thank you for that compliment, although obviously I fished for it," Gerry returned, smiling. "But won't you tell me, now that the draft has been ordered and your number called, how are you going to manage to escape? Of course I shall not speak to any one else of what you tell me."

"I am glad enough to tell you," Felipe Morris continued boyishly. "You can't imagine how hard it has been to have no one to sympathize with me. I have wished many times since war was declared that my mother was alive and I could have talked the situation over with her. My father, as I told you, is dead against me. He thinks I am a renegade and a disgrace to him and to his name, and a lot of stuff like that. It seems his brothers all fought in the Civil War and were officers and it has been the regret of his life he was too young. I wish he had the chance offered him now instead of me," he concluded like a surly boy, with all his gallantry departed.

"But what are you going to do?" Gerry insisted, her interest in him remaining so far unaffected by his attitude.

"Oh, I am too plagued healthy, so the doctor won't help me out. I hoped to be released on the score of ill health at first. But later I sent in a claim saying I could not be released for war service because I was the sole support of my parent and had to be left here to look after the ranch. I don't see why raising beans cannot be considered war work? Father insists he can run the place himself and I am afraid he won't stand by me when the exemption board asks him concerning the truth of my claim. Pretty tough when a fellow's own father is anxious to get him off his hands to the extent of possibly being killed."

Felipe laid his guitar down on the piazza and in spite of the fact that he must have been at least twenty-two or twenty-three years old, Gerry found herself with a ridiculous desire to comfort him.

"It is just a difference of opinion," she said softly. "I don't believe if I were you I would blame my father, and he should have the same respect for you. I never thought of the question before, but I have decided tonight I do not believe in the draft. Isn't there anything else you can do, if this one exemption claim fails?"

Felipe Morris rose up, shrugging his shoulders impatiently. He was so foreign in his appearance that the movement seemed natural.

"Oh, yes, I can slip away into Mexico and remain until the war is over. I have been thinking of it as a possibility. But of course if I am caught I shall be put into prison as a deserter."

Then he stood gazing down upon Gerry with a bewildered expression.

"I wonder why I have entrusted my fate to you in this fashion? You understand that if you should ever tell what I have confided to you, things would be all over with me."

Gerry also rose. "Shall we walk about your garden for a little?" she said. "I am tired of sitting still so long. I expect Mrs. Burton will be here in a little time and think we should go to bed. But you need not worry with regard to my ever mentioning a word of what you have said to me — not under any possible circumstances."

Then as they wandered about the tiny garden Felipe gathered a bunch of the small white and yellow roses.

"Keep these in your room tonight."

Afterwards discovering that Mrs. Burton and his father had returned to the garden and were coming toward them, he added hurriedly:

"Tell me, please, when and where I can see you again, alone? It has meant so much to me to be able to talk to you so freely and I have an idea we are going to be friends."

"But you have agreed to come over to our camp," Gerry answered, feeling at the same time that she would like selfishly to preserve Felipe's interest entirely for herself. Of course when he was introduced to the other Camp Fire girls he would naturally take less pleasure in her society.

"Oh, yes, indeed, I am coming to your camp. Anderson and I would not miss the opportunity for a good deal. But I want to see you by yourself, not with a dozen other people chattering around. Surely you can manage to make an engagement to see me alone. You would if you liked me half as much as I do you."

Again Felipe spoke like a spoiled boy, but Gerry had no time to reply, for at this instant Mrs. Burton and Mr. Morris reached them.

Truth to tell, she had a distinct sense of relief as, slipping her arm inside her Camp Fire guardian's, together they said their formal good-nights.

Already Felipe Morris was demanding more of Gerry than either of them realized.

CHAPTER IX

THE CANTONMENT

A few days after their visit at the ranch, arrangements were made for Mrs. Burton and members of her party to drive over to the new cantonment which was situated on a broad mesa not many miles away.

Gerry Williams announced that because of the dust and discomfort she preferred being left behind.

Sally Ashton also declined, stating that she was not well enough to consider undertaking the long drive and then being forced to walk about over whatever portion of the camp they were permitted to inspect. After her mishap, which Sally considered no one had regarded with sufficient seriousness, she had acquired a prejudice against excursions of any character.

Sally's attitude the Camp Fire guardian understood, although she was somewhat puzzled by Gerry Williams, as always before Gerry had been enthusiastic over change and excitement. One would have supposed that among all the girls she would have been most interested in the new war camp and the possibility of seeing and meeting the young American soldiers.

Mrs. Webster would not consider the trip, feeling that her heart would only be torn by the sight of so many war preparations, and more if she should chance to come in contact with an unusually homesick boy. Her sister could bring back word of whatever she could actually do to be of service, since often enough she was the pioneer who went forth in search of new ideas which Mrs. Webster put into execution.

Dan Webster was of course essential to the expedition, as he was chauffeur. Billy was not only invited, but Mrs. Burton insisted upon his accompanying them after he had very generously demurred, saying there was no reason why he should crowd the others when he really was not interested in war camps. She hoped, however, that the sight of the cantonment might exert either a mental or a spiritual influence upon him.

It was possible to manage eight in the car, although ordinarily it held but seven, yet one was willing to be a little inconvenienced under the circumstances, so the five girls, Vera Lagerloff, Bettina Graham, Alice Ashton, Marta Clark and Peggy Webster also accompanied Mrs. Burton.

The first part of the drive followed the now familiar line of the shore. Yet the outlook was never the same! Now and then one would see a heron or sand crane standing upon one leg near the water, apparently lost in immortal thought; sea gulls were dipping in and out, or else riding serenely on the waves; occasionally a buzzard, grim as Odin, soared overhead.

Once Marta Clark, who was on the front seat with Dan, gave a cry of surprise. She had discovered that what she supposed a great bird winging its flight over their car, was in reality an aeroplane on a long practice flight from North Island.

Finally leaving the coast, the automobile began a long climb over an undulating line of hills. The hills were bare except for occasional bunches of cacti and bushes of bright yellow tar weed. There were acres and acres of sage brush, sometimes a field of wild buckwheat and once in a while a small grove of live oak shrubs or of red and blue gum trees.

The mesa upon which the new cantonment was springing up like a magic city was a great desert of sand and sage. For years the thousands of acres had been of no use because of the lack of water. Now great irrigating ditches had been laid and the camp was being plentifully supplied with water by the city of San Diego.

The surroundings of the camp were cheerless enough, it is true, yet there was nothing cheerless in the atmosphere of the place itself. Even as the Camp Fire party approached they felt the undercurrent of the fine new force, the splendid vitality which the war has awakened in the world.

A sentry ordered Dan to stop his car within a few yards of the officers' quarters and Mrs. Burton was told that she must receive an official permit for their inspection of certain features of the camp.

From inside the little house, which looked like a miniature bungalow of unpainted pine, one heard the noise, not of the rattle of musketry, but the endless tip, tap, tap of many typewriters.

Captain Mason, who had been told of Mrs. Burton's intended visit, came out to greet her and her party.

He explained that just at present there were only a few hundred soldiers within the cantonment, although they were expecting many thousands within the next few weeks.

An army of workmen were at present engaged in preparing the way for the coming of the soldiers and the big artillery.

Strolling apart from the other laborers and still carrying a large hammer, Mr. Jefferson Simpson, the late Camp Fire guide, philosopher and friend, walked over to speak to Mrs. Burton and her companions. He offered no explanation for his presence at the camp, but it was obvious he had concluded that his efforts here were of more importance than his previous occupation. The Sunrise Camp Fire had always considered his remaining with them for so long a time an obvious absurdity and presumed that it was because of Mr. Simpson's continuing interest in Marie, although he had paid no attention to her since the breaking of their engagement.

But apparently his leading motive in life was to discover the number and variety of vocations in which he could engage.

After receiving a written order from the commanding officer for the day, Captain Mason led the way with Mrs. Burton walking beside him.

They were to be allowed to see only places of minor importance, the temporary tents and mess room, the Y. M. C. A. quarters. Mrs. Burton had explained that one of the chief reasons for their visit was a desire to find out how they might be of service in even the smallest possible way.

"You see, Captain Mason," she suggested, "we are living for the present not far behind the lines of this American war camp. In a different sense every woman and girl in our country should be a reserve soldier behind the lines until the war is over. One need not wear a uniform, or carry a gun to serve! Our American Camp Fire girls feel that they ought to be able to give as valuable service to the country as the Boy Scouts. I confess we have not yet altogether found our way."

By this time Mrs. Burton and Captain Mason had reached the Red Cross tent and now had paused for a moment outside to wait for the five girls and Dan and Billy Webster to join them.

Captain Mason nodded, waving his hand toward the open flap of the tent.

"You can help us keep our boys amused. I tell you that is the greatest problem we older officers have to meet with young, untrained soldiers. Discipline is comparatively easy, for few of the boys resent it; but look in there!"

Mrs. Burton did look, while Bettina and Marta and Peggy, who were nearest, also gazed in over her shoulders.

Several soldiers were sitting by a long board table looking at a pile of magazines, not because they were interested, but plainly because they had nothing else on earth they could think of to do.

On a raised platform a phonograph was playing an Italian love song. Some one must have started it, although at present no one apparently was listening to the music.

Several of the soldiers were writing letters, others were yawning and half lying down on the hard wooden benches, bored and listless and homesick.

Hearing voices outside the Y.M.C.A. tent, one young officer, who also had been writing, lifted his eyes.

The same instant Bettina Graham walked quickly inside the tent, holding out her hand.

56

"Why, here is my lieutenant!" she exclaimed. "May I call you my lieutenant, although Marta Clark will dispute the title? For I did reach you first after your accident and it is my first-aid treatment you seem to have survived. I did not know you had arrived at this cantonment, Lieutenant Carson. I do hope you have entirely recovered."

CHAPTER X
PLANS

One afternoon, after resting for an hour or more, Mrs. Burton appeared at her little front door, wondering why she was encompassed by so unusual a silence.

The fact that at present the Sunrise camp was situated several miles from any other human habitation, with the sea stretching before it and a great ranch as its background, did not ordinarily insure it an essential silence. As a matter of fact, there were generally nine youthful persons, engaged in strenuous occupations of one kind or another, in its immediate vicinity.

This afternoon Mrs. Burton discovered that they had withdrawn to some distance from the camping grounds.

A camp fire was burning and the girls were seated about it in ceremonial fashion, with Mrs. Webster also forming one of the group. A little further off her two sons were characteristically engaged, Dan in bringing small pieces of driftwood up from the shore and Billy in lying upon his back, gazing toward the sky.

In truth only their Camp Fire guardian appeared deliberately to have been left out of the gathering.

Mrs. Burton suffered a distinct sensation of aggrievement.

Evidently the Sunrise Hill Camp Fire girls were deep in a consultation of some important character, so that it seemed scarcely fair that they should have ignored her completely.

Not wishing to go back into her room, which had grown a little close, and yet not desiring to interrupt the proceedings, from which her presence had been so carefully excluded, Mrs. Burton hesitated a moment just outside her house. If she were seen wandering about nearby, as a matter of good manners she would have to be invited to the camp fire. With Mrs. Webster already there, she had not the excuse that her presence might be necessary. Often the girls seemed to prefer giving her sister their confidence.

At this instant one of the Camp Fire group observed her and gave the information to the others. Peggy began beckoning violently, while Bettina Graham and Marta Clark both jumped up and were coming toward her.

"You are lazy, Tante, we have been waiting for you to wake up for ages!" Bettina remarked, slipping her arm through the older woman's. She was several inches taller than her Camp Fire guardian, and oftentimes at a distance Mrs. Burton was mistaken for another girl, she was so slender and so youthfully and ardently alive both in body and spirit.

"Yes, you seem to have been tremendously anxious for my society," she returned in the voice and manner both Bettina and Peggy understood. If the other Camp Fire girls were at times a little in awe of their famous guardian, Peggy and Bettina appreciated that she was much like other persons and now and then behaved like a somewhat spoiled young girl. Certainly she never regarded her own achievements as placing her upon a pedestal.

From her present speech and manner Bettina realized that she was both jealous and hurt over their apparent disregard of her, for she had an almost ridiculous craving for affection as an ordinary human being, caring but little for the admiration which was a tribute to her as an artist rather than a woman.

Nevertheless Bettina laughed in an entirely unsympathetic fashion.

"Well, we did wish to discuss something before you put in an appearance, but now the discussion has been over for some time, we very much desire your society. Yet only if you are amiable, because just at this time it is enormously important that you should be."

Mrs. Burton frowned and then laughed, a little teased by Bettina's too evident understanding of her state of mind.

Marta Clark said nothing. She had not yet acquired the habit of regarding her Camp Fire guardian in any spirit save one of devoted admiration. But Marta was the latest of the group of Sunrise Camp Fire girls and of necessity knew her less well than the others. Moreover, Marta also dreamed of a future dramatic career and it was not so easy to take simply the one woman who personified her own ideals.

In the circle on the ground Peggy Webster had arranged a leather cushion ornamented with Camp Fire designs as a seat of honor for their guardian when she finally arrived.

Sitting down, Mrs. Burton clasped her hands over her knees, gazing curiously around.

"Is this a conspiracy or rebellion, or a plot?" she demanded. "It seems to me, Mollie Webster, not only because you are my sister, but because we alone belong to the same generation, that you at least should not have been one of the conspirators."

Like the proverbial Charlotte in "Wilhelm Meister," who went on cutting bread and butter, Mrs. Webster, without replying, continued knitting.

"Oh, our plot is not dangerous, or at least we do not think it is, although you may feel differently," Peggy Webster announced, to whom the task of imparting the information evidently had been awarded. "We have merely been discussing the idea of forming a Camp Fire branch to the War Camp Recreation League. You remember this League is to do whatever is possible for the entertainment of the soldiers and we talked of our share in it after our visit to the war camp the other day."

Mrs. Burton appeared slightly suspicious.

"I also remember, Peggy, that it was agreed I was to be allowed to choose what form our activities should take. Moreover, whatever plan presented itself to us was first to be submitted to an officer at camp to find out if the plan met with military approval. Camp Fire girls, however clever, are scarcely the proper persons to decide upon the ways and means for providing entertainment for our American soldiers, valuable as their aid may be in the entertainment itself. But there, forgive me, I do not intend being disagreeable, and I have no doubt you have thought up some thrilling scheme! Only why not wait until our little dinner party and dance for the soldiers tomorrow evening is over before we precipitate ourselves into a fresh undertaking?"

"Oh, our party is just a small matter compared to the plan we have been working out this afternoon," Peggy continued, refusing to be snubbed or argued into silence. "Our idea is that if we are to become a branch of the War Recreation Fund Committee we must raise money for the organization. We wish to give a play and present to the fund whatever money we make."

Mrs. Burton shook her head. "Give a play out here in this semi-wilderness? Well, the idea is agreeable enough if you wish to amuse yourselves, but how you expect to make money or secure an audience is beyond my imagination! However, if you have set your hearts upon the scheme and think it would amuse you, do as you like. I only ask to be left out altogether. Remember, I am resting from a histrionic career."

Mrs. Burton made a movement as if she contemplated leaving, but Peggy resolutely held her in her place.

"We do expect you to help; more, we expect you to be almost the entire thing!" Bettina interrupted with more vigor than clearness. "We are not contemplating a silly little amateur performance here at camp; we have more important things to interest us. We wish to give a real play at that exquisite open-air theater near the seaside resort that we saw the other day on our drive. Ever since then Marta and Peggy and I have been dreaming of little else and talking of little else to the other girls until now they are as enthusiastic as we are. It was Marta Clark who actually put our present scheme into our minds, and she merely spoke of how much she would enjoy seeing you act outdoors in so lovely a place."

"I am sure Marta is very kind," Mrs. Burton answered, but without revealing a profound appreciation of the compliment. "But don't be foolish, please. You know I try to do whatever is possible toward making our summers together happy and satisfying. Yet one of my chief reasons for living outdoors is to have a complete rest from my work and to get away from the whole thought of it as much as possible. I have given all the money to war causes I can afford at present. Later I shall do more, of course — — "

"That is just the point," Peggy interrupted. "If people out here in California learn you are to appear in an outdoor performance, they will positively flock to see you. You know you could earn a lot of money for the Recreation Fund, besides we all think it would be great fun to act with you and have already selected the play that would be the most interesting to produce."

"Really, Peggy, I think you have gone somewhat too far," Mrs. Burton answered, although with a slightly dazed expression. "I don't believe I have ever had a theatrical manager who made every arrangement, even to selecting the play in which I was to appear, without consulting me. The whole thing is preposterous. Mollie, I really cannot understand your allowing the girls to become so absorbed in such a nonsensical project! I think you might have spared me the difficulty of refusing."

"But you don't appear to be having any difficulty in refusing, Polly," Mrs. Webster answered with her usual placidity. Nevertheless, she realized how greatly this same placidity annoyed her beloved twin sister in moments of agitation. "Yet I am sorry that I agreed to permit the girls to broach the subject to you, since the idea seems to trouble you so much. Personally I am afraid I also found the idea charming. You have not acted for a long time and many of your friends are giving theatrical benefits for the Red Cross or some war need. The girls thought they would like to present 'As You Like It,' with you as Rosalind; you know you have played Rosalind dozens of times before. The open-air theater would make an exquisite

Forest of Arden. Besides, I am sure our present group of Camp Fire girls could not act, so poorly as you used to, now and then, in private theatricals in the old days. You know, my dear, none of us imagined then that you were to turn out a genius."

Mrs. Burton flushed. "No one imagines it now, Mollie." She answered with obvious irritability. Then her manner became more apologetic:

"You girls are not angry with me for refusing?"

Wisely Peggy shook her head, "No, we are only disappointed."

Then everybody in the little company remained silent for several moments, which was a most unusual state of affairs among the Sunrise Hill Camp Fire girls.

Plainly Mrs. Burton suffered from the depressing influence, for suddenly she got up.

"Please leave me alone for a little while. I must think the question over?" she announced, as if she had not already issued her ultimatum. The next moment she turned away and walked down toward the beach.

"What do you think Tante will decide, Mother?" Peggy anxiously inquired.

Mrs. Webster shook her head. "My dear, Polly and I are twins, and I have known her ever since I have known anything. But to tell beforehand how she will make up her mind upon any subject is beyond me. I am a little sorry we have made this request of her. She takes her work so seriously, and after all she is doing so much for us without the addition of this."

At this instant a cool voice was heard speaking in the background.

The voice was Billy Webster's.

"I believe Tante will have the time of her life acting with you girls, of course she will consent, although probably no one else on earth with her reputation would take such a risk."

CHAPTER XI

THE DANCE

The next day Mrs. Burton announced that having written her husband she would await his reply before reaching an absolutely definite decision in regard to their presentation of "As You Like It." In the meantime she insisted that the whole question of the performance be neither thought of nor discussed.

Appreciating that he had grown too old to make a valuable soldier and yet unwilling to be left out of war service, Mrs. Burton's husband, Richard Burton, had taken the necessary examinations and had received a commission in the Ordnance Department. He was now stationed at a southern camp.

Despite the Camp Fire guardian's request, there was a good deal of speculation among the girls concerning the possible outcome of their hopes. During the following day they were too much absorbed by the prospect immediately before them to give much time to the consideration of the future.

Having arranged a small dance and invited a number of soldiers from the nearby camp to be their guests, the girls had promised to do whatever work was necessary for their entertainment. This included the cooking of the party food as well as the other arrangements. But by this time, after several summers of camping life, each girl considered that she had become an artist in the preparation of one or more superior dishes.

Ordinarily the most indolent of the girls, on occasions of especial festivity Sally Ashton always assumed supreme command of the cooking. It was Sally who, with Gerry and Vera as her assistants, made both the bread and cake, articles of food of particular importance.

In the present ménu she was especially interested, as recently she had been experimenting with a number of new war recipes, finding them extremely successful. Now Sally wished to repeat the recipes for a larger company than their Camp Fire group.

Having by this time recovered from her accident, secretly Sally Ashton felt that she was being repaid for what she had suffered. She had secured a very agreeable new acquaintance, who showed the symptoms Sally so well understood of becoming one of her many admirers. The young man was Merton Anderson, who had been a guest at the Morris ranch and had ridden over to camp with the news of the accident.

Since then, with Mr. Morris and Felipe Morris, he had made several calls upon Mrs. Burton and ostensibly upon her group of Camp Fire girls. However, after Merton Anderson's first visit, Sally appreciated that the rest of his calls were due to her presence. No one could have explained how she managed, not even Sally herself, yet she had a fashion of seeing and conquering almost immediately both young men and old. No one ever observed her making an effort to attract attention. She was even unusually demure; nevertheless the attraction was going on in a subtle and scientific fashion.

Of Felipe Morris' attitude toward her, Gerry Williams was by no means so assured. Not since their original meeting at his home had she an opportunity of speaking to him alone, nor had she made the effort to secure such an opportunity. For some reason Gerry felt a certain shyness toward her new acquaintance, almost as if she were afraid of the influence he might be able to exert upon her.

Certainly she had no idea of making an appointment to meet him anywhere alone. Apart from the fact that Mrs. Burton would not approve, Gerry had been trained in a sufficiently hard school of experience to recognize the lack of wisdom in such a proceeding. If she wished Felipe to like her especially, and she was by no means sure at this time that she did wish it, then she must not allow herself to become cheapened in his eyes. Social conventions Gerry understood were of value and more especially to a girl in her position. However, Felipe had appeared to be courteous, although extraordinarily determined upon securing his own way.

In return for their kindness and also because she liked both young men, Mrs. Burton had invited Felipe Morris and Merton Anderson to their Camp Fire entertainment. The entertainment was to be more than an ordinary dance, since the guests had been invited to a swimming party in the afternoon, then dinner and the dance later.

Since the girls were to spend a portion of the afternoon in swimming, most of the preparations for their party necessarily had to be made beforehand. Mrs. Webster had promised to look after final details, and also there was Marie, who was temperamental, but who could be relied upon to accomplish marvels when she was in the proper mood. Since the entry of the United States into the war, Marie, who was an ardent French woman, had adopted the American soldier as her especial protégé.

Moreover, on the morning before their dance Alice Ashton and Peggy Webster had motored into town, purchasing the provisions they considered too troublesome to prepare. They bought two roast hams and a roast of beef and half a dozen varieties of fruit. Their ménu was to consist of cold meats, baked beans, which were a Camp Fire speciality, roast potatoes and corn, which could be cooked over the outdoor fire, cornbread, fruit salad, coffee and cake.

In the afternoon the girls were to wear their Camp Fire bathing suits, but at night they had concluded to appear in white dresses, with their honor beads, almost as beautiful and as effective as jewels.

The ceremonial Camp Fire costumes were somewhat too heavy and too warm for dancing on a midsummer night in a semi-tropical land.

The girls were naturally a trifle shy over the prospect of guests, nearly all of whom were complete strangers. Among them were only two with whom they had any previous acquaintance. They were Lieutenant Geoffrey Carson and Private George Ferguson, the soldiers who were aided after an accident in their motor car, by the Camp Fire girls during their riding trip down the coast.

Two of the soldiers were members of one of the regimental bands and had promised to play for the dancers, since the girls possessed only a much-used victrola and were too far off in the country to be able to engage the services of professional musicians.

No dance could have been less conventional, when for one thing the white, smooth sands of the beach below the camp were to serve as the ballroom floor.

Truly here indeed were the colors of romance, the moon and the sea, youth and a wind-swept shore!

That night, dancing with Felipe Morris, Gerry believed that she had never been so happy.

With his Southern ancestry and musical gifts, naturally Felipe was a wonderful dancer, possessing an almost perfect sense of rhythm and time.

On one occasion Gerry and Felipe discovered that they were actually dancing alone, their companions having stopped for a moment to watch them. Then they were only brought to a realization of what had taken place by hearing Mrs. Burton cry: "Bravo!" and afterwards the applause of a dozen pairs of hands.

A little while before Felipe had lifted their right arms and he and Gerry had danced in and out in semi-circles until they formed the petals of a flower; reaching the center they revolved slowly in a circle, until almost ceasing to move.

Mrs. Burton decided that seldom had she seen a more enchanting picture — Gerry with her delicate blonde prettiness, Felipe Morris so complete a contrast. But then a great deal may have been due to the effect of the outdoor scene and the moonlight!

Before midnight, after dancing for several hours and after their long afternoon swim, the dancers must have grown weary, for they wandered off and sat down in little groups on the sand.

This was Gerry's and Felipe's opportunity, for at once Felipe led her to a place where they were in sight of the others and yet where they could not be overheard.

The rock Felipe had chosen rose above an amethyst carpet of sea verbena where Gerry sat enthroned while he lay down on the floral carpet.

Felipe could adopt an attitude of careless grace with more assurance than the usual American youth. Indeed, he looked utterly unlike any of the other young men who were the guests of the Camp Fire girls this night.

They wore their uniforms and were bronzed and fit.

At this time the soldiers of the National Guard were beginning slowly to fill their new military camps, as they were to be the first regiments ordered to France after the regular army had crossed. The drafted men were not yet ready for service. During this memorable first summer, after the entry of the United States into the war, the lists of the drafted men were being prepared with great difficulty.

Therefore no one of the soldier guests questioned Felipe Morris' position. It was presumed that he and Merton Anderson were in the attitude of waiting for their call to the colors.

Among the small company only Gerry and Mrs. Burton and Merton Anderson were aware of Felipe's attempt to claim exemption. Naturally the matter was not one that he cared to discuss with strangers, and more especially not with young men near his own age, who had volunteered rather than wait for the drafting.

However, Felipe was at present pleasantly sure of Gerry's sympathy.

"Fine looking soldiers, our American warriors!" he began in a lazy, good-humored tone, which nevertheless held a slight suggestion of disparagement. "I suppose one ought to rejoice that there are some men among us who have the masculine passion for fighting so long as the Kaiser's Huns are still abroad in the world. But personally I don't feel I should make a success as a soldier."

Such a conversation would not have made the slightest impression upon any one of the Sunrise Hill Camp Fire girls except Gerry.

It was obvious that Felipe preferred some one else to shoulder his responsibility and do his duty. Selfishness is neither original nor unique!

But Gerry was not given to deep reflection and was already more under her companion's influence than she realized.

"When are we going to have a meeting together somewhere off to ourselves?" Felipe asked. "There are so many things I want to talk to you about; it is tantalizing to see you for only a few moments at a time now and then. Why can't you come over and stay again at the ranch? My father does nothing but read war news all day and either Shakespeare or Cervantes in the evening, so we would be virtually alone."

The prospect sounded alluring to Gerry, nevertheless she slowly shook her head.

"I should like it, of course," she answered, smiling and showing her small but very regular white teeth, "only, like a good many other pleasant things in this world, it is out of the question for me. I cannot stay at your home alone with just your father and yourself. Besides, your father would never think of inviting me, and although I should enjoy seeing you alone at some other time, I am afraid even that is impossible. Mrs. Burton would not — —"

Here Felipe laughed in a teasing fashion.

"Is this the vaunted freedom of the American girl? I thought only the other evening you confided to me that you had always been forced to depend upon yourself ever since you were a little girl and that there had been no one in your life who had ever influenced your decisions! Now you speak of Mrs. Burton as if you were a tiny school girl. Let me assure you — if assurance be necessary—that I intended nothing wicked or even unconventional. I only wished you to take a walk with me some afternoon, or a sail. I have a motor boat, and there are hours when the sea is not rough. As a matter of fact, I meant to ask Mrs. Burton's permission, in case I had your consent first. Mrs. Burton strikes me as a charming person and not one who would be too strict a chaperon. Naturally, as I have spent all my life in this neighborhood, I know the attractive parts of the country."

Felipe's tone was not so much annoyed as it was patronizing, and Gerry accepted it in this spirit.

She disliked making social mistakes, and she had had so little social training and experience that she was apt to regard her mistakes as of more importance than they actually were.

Now she supposed that she had misunderstood Felipe from the beginning and that her own stupidity had been at fault. So she replied somewhat humbly:

"I am sorry. If Mrs. Burton is willing, of course I shall enjoy walking or sailing with you. But don't let me keep you away from the other girls too long tonight. Suppose we walk over and join Mrs. Burton."

As if she intended rising, Gerry made a slight movement. Her companion did not stir.

"Sit down, please, I am afraid you are angry," he returned. "I do wish I had my guitar with me; I should like to sing to you. Mrs. Burton asked me to bring it over tonight, but I had rather not sing before the others."

So Gerry stayed on and allowed Felipe to talk, while she said little in reply, only glancing now and then from the figure at her feet to the beauty of the moonlit ocean. Vaguely she wondered why she had always been convinced she did not care for the outdoor world. It was stupid never to have realized its loveliness until tonight!

But, while Gerry and Felipe were having their talk together, only a short distance away Lieutenant Geoffrey Carson and Bettina Graham were engaged in a very different character of conversation.

It chanced that Lieutenant Carson, who was a Virginian, had an uncle who had been a representative in Congress for a number of years. Having visited his uncle, Lieutenant Carson had not only heard of Bettina's distinguished father, but had met him and knew of his effort to persuade his country to take her high place among the nations in the fight for a world-wide democracy.

So, since Bettina Graham's father was her idol, she experienced none of her customary shyness in talking to the young National Guard officer. She had liked him in their former meetings, not resenting his quiet sense of humor, a contrast to her own seriousness.

"Then you are in absolute sympathy with our having entered the war, Lieutenant Carson?" Bettina inquired, adding: "I think I always have been—and yet now and then one cannot help feeling that all war must be wrong."

Before the young officer could reply, they heard some one approaching and glancing up Bettina discovered Billy Webster.

The next moment, without awaiting their invitation, Billy took a seat on the sands beside them.

Bettina was not surprised, for few persons who knew Billy intimately continued to be surprised by his unexpected actions. Indeed, they would have been surprised had he behaved otherwise. Now, although Bettina was a little annoyed at having her conversation interrupted, she made no effort to interfere with his intention.

The turning of Billy Webster from the accomplishment of his desire required a tremendous amount of energy which the result scarcely ever justified.

So far as Lieutenant Carson was concerned, because Billy looked so much younger than he actually was, he regarded him merely as a presuming small boy.

Moreover, at the beginning of their talk, certainly Billy behaved like one. First he stared at Lieutenant Carson's dress uniform, with the single bar on his collar and sleeve and then up into the officer's firm, smooth-shaven face. Finally, leaning over close to his companion, he fastened his large visionary blue eyes upon the officer's steadfast brown ones.

"Why did you do it?" Billy inquired. Then, because he was accustomed to being compelled to explain himself, he continued: "I mean why did you volunteer, why go through all the hard work and rigmarole to be appointed an officer in the army? You look as if you had an unusual lot of sense, so I cannot imagine that you do not understand there are finer things to do with one's life than killing people. I should think you could see how much more men are called upon to conquer poverty and injustice and the crime that comes of it, than they are called upon to conquer one another. Of course if you had been drafted that would have been a different matter. Most people do what other people tell them to do. That is why I believe if all the leaders of the world would preach peace, all war would end."

Instead of appearing to take the youthful pacifist seriously, Lieutenant Carson smiled. Billy was a little offensive and misguided, nevertheless there was something interesting about the boy; he had such an intense manner, such an appearance of being convinced of his own point of view. And Billy's personality suggested the thinker, not the man of action.

"Then you are under the impression we are over there in our encampment for the fun of it and in order to kill time which we might be spending in better ways?" he inquired, thinking that perhaps he might answer Bettina's anxious questionings and Billy's impertinence at the same time. "Well, as a matter of fact, our encampment is not a very attractive place up to the present. Did you think so when you made us the visit? One job we have been tackling recently is to clear away the underbrush from a good many

72

thousands of acres of desert which have remained undisturbed from the year one until now. We killed ninety rattlesnakes as a part of the first day's work. Later on we are going to drive artillery across those wastes of sand. Does not sound like play, does it?"

"No," Billy returned patiently, wondering why people would not sometimes answer his questions directly, without first preaching long sermons which seemed to have but little bearing upon them.

"It is because I think a soldier's life is so hard and must be so distasteful to a lot of men that I wonder why you would rather give your energy to fighting than to trying to make the world happier and wiser in other ways."

Lieutenant Carson frowned. He knew the things Billy was saying were being said by a good many people the world over, who were older and wiser, or who should have been wiser, than Billy. But he also realized that these same sentiments were not easy to answer, because they had in them so much of the germ of truth, which was to blossom and flower at some future day.

Moreover, unexpectedly he experienced an impulse to help the boy to see the present world struggle in a clearer light.

"Billy," he added, "you will agree with me, won't you, that pretty nearly everybody is saying the same thing these days? We all claim that we wish the world to enjoy universal peace, that we long for greater justice and happiness and a deeper sense of brotherhood. There is only one point that divides you and me just at present. We all want peace, but some of us want it so much that we are willing to pay for it by the final last sacrifice of our youth and our blood. There are others who think it may be obtained, and apparently you are one of them, simply by sitting still and talking the whole subject over. This is pretty difficult as things are at present. So long as the devil is such a scrapper, those of us who believe in the triumph of right have got to learn to fight back harder and even more successfully than he can fight."

Billy was silent for a moment, then with an egotism which was eminently characteristic, he remarked: "Well, perhaps that is the way some people must see the thing. Do you know I have always believed that some day I am going to have a tremendous influence upon people just through talking to them."

Then, by the time Lieutenant Carson had recovered from his surprise at Billy's audacity, he had made up his mind that the hour had arrived for their return to camp.

CHAPTER XII

"AS YOU LIKE IT"

The more Mrs. Burton dwelt upon the idea of giving a play for the recreation fund of the soldiers, the more the idea pleased her. Upon going more deeply into the subject she discovered that an effort was being made to secure funds for the building of a theater in each war camp in the United States.

To initiate the movement and to be the first contributor to the fund here in their immediate neighborhood, Mrs. Burton realized would give her great pleasure. If her fellow players were offering to act at these theaters, traveling from one to the other in a regular circuit during the coming winter, then surely the theaters should be provided!

Moreover, after having first suffered a natural objection to acting with novices, Mrs. Burton changed her point of view to the extent of considering that it might be rather charming to play with her own Camp Fire girls in a comedy fresh and sparkling as Shakespeare's "As You Like It." The play itself was in the spirit of a summer vacation, full of the outdoors and delicious improbabilities. Besides the effort would be a valuable experience for her Camp Fire girls.

Captain Burton had written, expressing not only his approval of the suggestion, but a real enthusiasm, provided Mrs. Burton felt well enough to undertake it. Also he suggested that Mrs. Burton find some professional actor in California who would play Orlando to her Rosalind. Then the contrast between her acting and that of her amateur company need not be so conspicuous. He also proposed that she secure the assistance of a professional stage manager to assist in the training of her players.

In the beginning of their discussion concerning the production of "As You Like It," Mrs. Burton had announced as insurmountable the obstacle that the cast required a greater number of men than of women characters. It

75

appeared that the girls already had considered this fact and were prepared with a proposal.

Peggy and Bettina had talked the matter over quietly with Lieutenant Carson on the night of their dance, begging him not to speak of it if nothing came of their idea. But they were thus able to report that Lieutenant Carson believed his commanding officer would permit a few of the soldiers to act with them in "As You Like It," provided the rehearsals did not interfere with their army work.

Later, when the performance became an actual possibility, Lieutenant Carson inquired among his soldier companions until he discovered the men who had some past dramatic experience and would also be acceptable in a social way.

Besides the soldiers Mrs. Burton later on invited Felipe Morris and Merton Anderson to become members of her cast.

Merton Anderson declined. No one knew the reason for his refusal except Sally Ashton, who, as a matter of fact, had begged him not to take part. Personally she did not approve of the outdoor play and had no idea of making the effort necessary to portray the least important character. Therefore Sally did not wish her latest admirer to become involved in an interest which would separate him from her society.

Felipe Morris appeared delighted to take part, and it was his aid which Mrs. Burton desired. She was confident that he would be able to act with unusual grace and self-assurance for a novice, and at least he possessed good looks and a naturally artistic temperament.

Moreover, Mrs. Burton and Felipe's father had become good friends, so that she believed that Mr. Morris would be pleased to have Felipe drawn into an intimate association with certain of the soldiers of the National Guard, trusting that they might influence him. Personally Mrs. Burton thought the one thing necessary was to entice Felipe away from his music and his indolent dreaming into the world of real men where he would awaken to his duty.

She knew of his friendship with Gerry and of the somewhat marked interest they apparently felt in each other, but she did not take the fact seriously. Already he had asked several times that he and Gerry be allowed to spend an afternoon together and Mrs. Burton had promptly consented. No longer did she cherish the illusion that she could hide away her Camp Fire girls in even the remotest corners of the globe without their being discovered. Therefore, after her foolish alarm over Bettina and her unconventional Indian friendship, she had concluded not to be so nervous a second time, but to trust to the discretion of the girls themselves.

Among the seven Camp Fire girls Gerry was exceptionally pretty and so could not fail to receive attention. But not for a single moment did Mrs. Burton dream that there was anything more than a superficial attraction between Gerry and Felipe. Of course she considered Gerry too young, not realizing that Felipe Morris was four years her senior and that Gerry's history had made her older than most girls of her age.

Yet after the verdict was reached and the actors secured, there still remained many details to be settled, the most important being the selection of the characters for the production of the Shakespearean comedy. Then, although there was a good deal of discussion, and Mrs. Burton allowed a free expression of opinion, in each choice she remained the court of final decision.

It was she who at the beginning of the discussion settled upon Marta Clark for the character of Celia, sweet cousin to Rosalind and second only in importance. In consequence Marta, who had not expected the honor, suffered a confusion of emotions, surprise, pleasure, alarm! Mrs. Burton had not forgotten their absurd first meeting, nor Marta's shy confession of an ambition to follow in her footsteps. If she had ability — and it was more than probable since her brother had lately written a clever play showing a dramatic gift in the family — Mrs. Burton had every intention of aiding

Marta in her desire when the right moment arrived. This would be but a slight return in memory of the friend who so generously had helped her in the old days.

Moreover, Mrs. Burton felt that she and Marta must learn to know each other better. To play beside her as Celia, to be with each other constantly at rehearsals would not only afford her the chance to test Marta's talent, but would give them an opportunity to become better friends.

Marta possessed vivacity, a love of poetry and of nature; these things Mrs. Burton had found out. Also her face depended upon the passing mood for its charm, a superior gift to beauty in an emotional actress.

Gerry Williams and Peggy were to impersonate Phebe, a shepherdess, and Audrey, a country wench, after a good-natured argument in which Peggy insisted upon this division of honors because of Gerry's superior prettiness.

Touchstone, the gay clown in "As You Like It," sings several of the most charming ballads in all Shakespeare. Because of his beautiful voice and his grace as a dancer Mrs. Burton begged Felipe Morris to play Touchstone, and he appeared pleased to accept.

Lieutenant Carson agreed to portray Jaques, whose soliloquy, "All the world's a stage," is one of the greatest speeches in English literature.

Dan Webster determined upon the character of Adam, servant to Orlando, while Billy Webster together with Sally Ashton refused to show the slightest interest in the approaching performance.

The other members of the cast were the officers and soldiers from the nearby cantonment. They expressed a great deal of enthusiasm over the relief the rehearsals afforded from the hard physical labor of these early days of their army training. Moreover, they would not even attempt to express their pleasure in associating so informally with a number of agreeable girls.

Bettina, Alice and Vera Lagerloff were to be ladies-in-waiting at the court of the Duke.

If Sally Ashton's refusal to play any part was due to her inherent indolence, Billy's lack of interest was ascribable to the wholly opposite cause.

Now and then for a passing moment when she had time to think of her always erratic nephew, Mrs. Burton wished that Billy had been yielding to his usual slothfulness. But recently he had awakened to an amazing energy and was working as he never had worked in his life.

After his brief conversation with Lieutenant Carson, for no reason which he chose to explain, Billy proceeded to find out whatever was possible in regard to the details of the new war camps. The monthly magazines and newspapers to which his aunt, or any one else at Sunrise camp subscribed, he searched diligently for all war information. Then he would disappear on long walks, announcing on his return that he had been over in the direction of the new National Guard cantonment, following the railroad tracks which had recently been laid from the city.

Finally he imparted the surprising information that he had secured work as a day laborer at the war camp, Mr. Jefferson Simpson having vouched for him. Moreover, Billy declared that he had given his aunt's name as a security for his trustworthiness and that Captain Mason had remembered his original visit to camp with Mrs. Burton's party.

Of Billy's value as a day laborer his family and friends felt extremely uncertain. But Billy explained that he was only expected to stand around and to hand the carpenters who were at work the tools they happened to need at the moment. He also carried buckets of water back and forth and in short did whatever chores he was ordered to do.

Mrs. Webster and Peggy were touched by Billy's unexpected display of patriotism, knowing how abhorrent labor of this kind had always been to him. Never, except under absolute coercion, had Billy ever performed the slightest manual work upon their own farm!

Mrs. Burton, Dan Webster and even the usually trustful Vera were not so enthusiastic over Billy's latest departure. Without confessing the fact, they suffered vague discomfort.

What possible plan had Billy in mind? If one only could believe he had chosen this method of "doing his bit!" But this would have been a commonplace attitude, and Billy was never commonplace.

There were moments when Mrs. Burton wondered if Billy were intent upon preaching his childish ideas upon pacifism and had chosen the one place where they would be most troublesome and dangerous! However, she was too deeply absorbed in making a success of the play which she and the Camp Fire girls had undertaken to allow much time to the consideration of her nephew.

The Camp Fire girls were learning to know their guardian in a new light. Under ordinary circumstances she was extremely lenient and more than willing to allow them to do as they liked.

But now they were to see her not in a holiday mood, but as an artist at work at her task. Since they had insisted upon the production of "As You Like It," the penalty rested upon them. Therefore she would suffer no idleness and accept no excuses for delay or carelessness.

At one of the rehearsals, Peggy having appeared uncertain of her lines, was publicly lectured and sent back to her tent with the suggestion that if she were unwilling to do her duty, some one else had best take her place.

CHAPTER XIII

HUMAN PSYCHOLOGY

Billy Webster, who had difficulty in living peacefully and happily with the people in his own walk of life, possessed a curious genius for making himself popular with the so-called "working classes."

At first the workmen at the new National Guard camp paid no especial attention to the delicate looking boy who suddenly appeared among them. But in a short time Billy proved unexpectedly useful.

For one thing he made no effort to talk. He merely stood about in places where he thought he might be of service, doing what he was told and asking no questions. Several times he displayed an intelligent initiative. And when each man is trying to do the work of two or three, every small saving of unnecessary effort through some one else counts.

At the present time there were fifteen hundred laborers employed on the cantonment. They were building barracks and small wooden bungalows and large store-houses for provisions and supplies from the ordnance and quartermaster departments. Every hour or so freight had to be unloaded from cars, so that they might be removed from the tracks and others take their place.

The soldiers were more often employed in the construction of roads and the clearing away of a century's growth of underbrush.

There was little in the camp that escaped Billy's quiet observation. The very fact that he did not talk, when ordinarily he had a passion as well as a gift for conversation was in itself a suspicious circumstance.

For once in his life Billy was finding it more worth while to listen and receive information rather than to impart his own ideas.

At first the great drawback was that the laborers did not have time, or else they did not feel the inclination to talk at all seriously. They would simply exchange jokes with one another, or sing snatches of popular songs.

The laborers belonged to a company under bond to the government that there would be no traitors employed at the war camps. Therefore if the men held any views connected with the war, they gave no expression to them. Moreover, the officers and soldiers were constantly in and out among the men at all hours. Nevertheless, Billy became more and more convinced that if a man were willing to sacrifice his own life in case he were discovered, it was impossible even with the strictest regulations to avoid the peril of a spy.

One day at lunch time the boy was sitting alone in the shadow made by a pile of lumber, which afforded a little relief from the heat of the noon sun, when two of his fellow laborers came and sat down only a few feet away. They saw him, of course, but seemed not to resent his presence; so, after smiling with the innocent, boyish expression peculiar to him, Billy continued eating. He brought his lunch with him every day in a basket as the other laborers did.

One of the two men, whom he thought a Swede, was rather an especial friend, although the only fashion in which they so far had expressed their friendliness was by smiling whenever they met.

He was a dull, good-natured fellow, blond and mild of manner. "Seems a pity to have to bring all these boys away from their homes and their mothers and sweethearts to plant them down in this desert in the heat of summer," he remarked to his companion, after he had bitten off a large hunk of sour bread and was slowly chewing on it like a cud. Finally, taking out his soiled handkerchief, he wiped the perspiration from his forehead.

"I have not been in the West very long, and it is sure enough God's country?" the blond workman went on. "But what a lot of waste land waiting for men to water and then plough and sow it! I thought all this desert land was soon to be redeemed and now all the young men have to go away from their own country into another land to fight. Sometimes it's a hard thing for a dull, common man to understand the good of war."

Billy stopped eating and slid over a few feet nearer. His blue eyes were beginning to shine.

"Wouldn't it be great if each man who has pledged his life to serve his country would do some deed which would save life instead of taking it?" he demanded. Then Billy paused and grew hot and cold by turns. He was not very sure of what he was trying to argue except in a vague fashion, and there was something about his last remark which held a suggestion of treason. He did not intend being disloyal. It was only that his preconceived ideas of right and wrong had been greatly troubled by the present war, and Billy was not willing to accept conditions as he found them, possessing the spirit which must solve its own problems.

He reddened as he found his new acquaintances staring at him suspiciously.

"Then you think peace brings the great mass of the people better fortune than war?" asked the other man, who had been quiet until now. He was a little, dark man, probably of Italian origin.

Billy hesitated. "I don't know," he answered, "I only believe peace should make men wiser and kinder to each other. But recently everything has gotten so dreadfully mixed in my mind, I can't be sure of anything. Perhaps I am mistaken."

"War has to be, young man," Billy's mild-mannered friend announced, nodding his head.

"Yes, that is what everybody says," the boy agreed.

Then the somewhat pointless conversation was obliged to end, as the hour for lunch had passed.

Among the experiences which Billy Webster was particularly enjoying at this time were his long walks back and forth from the place where he was spending his nights to the scene of his daily labors.

For, literally, he only spent his nights at the Sunrise camp. He arrived at home after the others had finished dinner, and rose and went away each morning just after daylight. But instead of the long, fatiguing walks, added to the unusual work of the war camp, injuring Billy's health—never had he appeared so strong and well.

Not that any one, aside from his mother, was paying particular attention to Billy's vagaries. Even Vera Lagerloff, for the first time in their long friendship, temporarily was neglecting Billy's welfare in her enthusiasm over the approaching production of "As You Like It."

However, Billy rejoiced in his new freedom.

He took pleasure in slipping out of his tent in the early morning, leaving Dan still asleep. Then he would prepare his own breakfast of coffee, fruit and eggs which were always left where he could readily find them. Afterwards, with his basket of lunch that his mother made ready the night before, Billy would move quietly off.

Even the dawns in this southwestern world were unlike the dawns Billy remembered in his own New Hampshire hills. Not that he would have claimed the New Hampshire hills as his possession because of a mere accident of birth. Billy cared infinitely more for the softness, the warmth and strangeness of this new country and climate than he had ever cared for the austerity of New England. It was awakening in him new strength and new purposes which so far he scarcely understood.

The way the dawn broke here in the western coast Billy particularly loved; it was so serene. There was not the drear, melancholy darkness and then the swift coming of light. But first a pearl-gray mist covered the sky, afterwards lavender and rose shone behind it and finally a pure gold, with the ocean as a mirror of the sky.

A part of the trip he could make by street car, nevertheless this left many miles to be traveled at either end of the line.

However, as Billy wished to think things out for himself, these walks afforded a wonderful opportunity. The difficulty of his life had always been due to his refusal to accept any judgment except his own. He honestly could not understand why his family even thought they had the right to interfere with him. Yet now he was up against the great fact of human discipline, the law which so often forces us to submit to a higher power.

The boys at the National Guard camp were not much older than himself, at least some of them were not. Nevertheless they were engaged upon tasks which he knew must be hard and distasteful and were prepared to face far worse things later on. Some of them had thought the question over for a long time, nearly three years in fact, until they were prepared to fight the enemy, body and soul, to a finish. Others of the soldiers were not given to thinking, but were obeying a good fighting instinct. All of them, however, were acknowledging an authority higher than their own and obeying a higher will.

Often Billy wondered how he should feel if the war lasted long enough to make the same demand upon him? Would he give up his belief in peace and the unrighteousness of war to serve as a common soldier in the ranks? And even if he did do this, was it in him to make a good soldier, to sacrifice himself for a common cause? Sometimes Billy prayed to be delivered from the test.

Yet whatever his own mental problems, there was one big fact of which Billy became daily more assured and that was his tremendous personal admiration for the new National Guard soldiers. Certainly theirs was the road of heroism and self-sacrifice, while the pacifists, even if right in principle, were skulking behind the protection the soldiers gave to them.

There were moments when Billy became a little scornful of the pacifists, himself included, who preferred the easiest way.

Ordinarily the boy took his long tramps to and from camp alone, but on the day after his brief conversation with the two workmen, the men joined him at the close of the day, walking for a short distance one on either side. Billy felt absurdly proud, as if the men at last regarded him as one of them. They even spoke of labor unions in his presence and Billy was glad to announce that he approved of unions.

Afterwards, perhaps four or five days later, Billy did not return to the Sunrise camp, even at the comparatively late hour which had become his habit.

Mrs. Webster suffered a good deal of uneasiness. Billy explained that he had been compelled to go into the nearest town on important business, so she was not to worry. One could scarcely say beforehand what demands war work might make upon one's time and strength.

Mrs. Webster steeled herself to bear the strain, even when Billy's new passion for helping to win the war kept him away from the Sunrise camp until nearly midnight for several nights in succession.

Just at this time she was extremely busy assisting with the preparation of the costumes for the Sunrise Camp Fire production of "As You Like It." In spite of the fact that Mrs. Burton had sent east for several trunks of costumes, there were many alterations to be made, and every member of the entire cast, maid and man, asked of Mrs. Webster either advice or aid, or both.

No matter how great her weariness, Mrs. Webster always remained awake until her son's return, in order that she might know he was well and have him eat a carefully saved-over dinner.

Gently Billy endeavored to persuade his mother to give up this plan, insisting that he always had food in town. But although Mrs. Webster made no effort to interfere with his actions, on this one point she was adamant. She must be sure that her son was safely at camp in order to be able to sleep.

Realizing this to be true, for several nights Billy returned to camp at the usual time. Then a night arrived when he reached home even later than before.

It chanced that on this night, without Billy's being aware of the fact, Mrs. Burton and her cast had been going through a dress rehearsal of their play.

When Billy finally reached camp, the Sunrise Hill tents were dark and still.

Yet to the left a camp fire was burning and a woman's figure was seated near it.

A pang of remorse stirred Billy, in spite of his own weariness.

Coming forward with his arms outstretched, instead of his mother, he discovered Vera Lagerloff.

"Goodness, Vera, I never saw you look so wonderful!" Billy exclaimed, bowing with the air of a courtier and a grace which he knew well how to assume.

For Vera was wearing a court costume, a skirt of a deep rose-colored satin and a polonaise and basque of white with a design of roses.

Her dark hair was piled high on her head and her cheeks were slightly rouged, since every preparation for the actual stage performance had been made.

Billy had never seen Vera so handsome, nor dreamed it possible that she could ever look as she did tonight. But then Billy had thought little of Vera's appearance, or of that of any other girl. He had simply cared for her with a curious boyish selfishness and affection. Unconsciously he always planned his future with Vera beside him to hear of his trials and conquests, but had never thought of how this could be managed.

Yet tonight Vera paid no attention to his unusual flattery.

Her expression suggested annoyance and reproach.

"Wait here, Billy, I'll find you something to eat. I made your mother go to bed and she and Mrs. Burton agreed that I might wait for you."

But Billy would not let her go. "I'm not hungry, Vera. Besides you look like a queen, not a kitchen maid. What's up? Fire away."

"That is what I wish to have you tell me," Vera returned, with the deep and abiding gentleness, which usually overcame Billy's obstinacy where other people and other methods failed.

He laughed. "I thought as much. Nothing doing, Vera. I am not going to tell anybody anything. Yes, I know I promised not to get into mischief again, after that last escapade of mine. But what did it amount to, going to jail for a little while, it was merely an interesting experience!"

Billy took Vera's hand in his own almost equally slender one, since Vera's was the hand of a peasant ancestry and Billy's the opposite.

"See here, dear, I am not sorry to have you and mother and Tante begin worrying about me, fearing I am going to do something foolish. You never seem to think me capable of anything else. But this time, between you and me, Vera, if I could tell you what is interesting me right now — and I confess it is not only my work at the war camp, although it has a close connection — well, I don't believe you would consider me foolish."

"Then, why won't you tell me what is interesting you, Billy? You know I don't always think ideas are foolish, but oftentimes I don't think your judgment wise. Besides, I am afraid something may happen to you!"

Billy shook his head, still holding her hand with boyish affection.

"These are war times, Vera. You and I used to disagree on the subject — one of the first questions we have ever seriously disagreed upon since we were little children. Anyhow, what I am interested in at present has something to do with the war. I cannot tell you details, as I must not confide in any one just now. Only promise me you'll see that mother does not worry and that neither she nor Tante makes a scene to try to force me into giving up my present work. I should simply go on with it anyhow, Vera."

Vera sighed. The problem of Billy Webster had always been too much for other people. Was he in the future to become a problem too big for her?

CHAPTER XIV

THE NIGHT OF THE PLAY

During the weeks of rehearsal before the performance of "As You Like It," the Camp Fire girls and the young officers and soldiers from the National Guard camp had delightful opportunities for developing new friendships.

When the emotion which existed between Felipe Morris and Gerry Williams became more than an ordinary friendship, the chances for exchanging confidences were more frequent than one would readily guess.

Felipe possessed a talent for pursuing the ends he desired in a quiet, unostentatious fashion. There were moments when merely passing by Gerry with other people near, he would whisper a few words which only she could hear. Then, when neither of them expected to be called for their share in a rehearsal, they used to slip away together to some secluded place for more intimate conversations.

The final rehearsals took place at the open-air theater near one of the most fashionable seaside resorts in southern California, and Felipe was familiar with the coast and the surrounding country.

There were no long, dull waits for them between the moments when they were actually upon the stage, no sense of fatigue and boredom of which the other amateur players occasionally complained.

Gerry appeared to be happy to listen and Felipe to talk to her indefinitely.

Of course the other actors were aware of Gerry's and Felipe's interest in each other and tried teasing them now and then, but since neither denied the fact, the effort lost its piquancy.

Nor were Mrs. Burton and Mrs. Webster entirely blind, although they did not accept the situation seriously. It was ridiculous to presume that every friendship between a girl and a man must be regarded with solemnity. Nevertheless it is more than possible that if Mrs. Burton had not been so absorbed in the coming performance she would have noticed some tell-tale circumstances. Her extreme preoccupation was her chief excuse.

She did mention to her sister several times that she never had seen Gerry look so pretty or appear as happy as she had for the past few weeks.

"Why, the child is like a field of wild flowers; her hair is the color of buttercups, her eyes are cornflowers and her cheeks — —"

But here Mrs. Burton's flow of imagery had been stopped by Mrs. Webster's protest.

"Please don't be so absurd, Polly. You know conversation of that character merely strikes me as foolish." So Mrs. Burton had laughed and the subject of Gerry was dismissed.

Gerry was becoming aware of a change in her own life, not in her mere appearance, but in a way far deeper. There were moments when she even hoped her own drab, lonely existence was past forever and that a life as radiant as these past weeks would endure. She tried not to hope too much from Felipe's manner and the kind things he said to her now and then. Of course she was too young for him to think of seriously. Nevertheless Gerry could not refrain from occasionally seeing a happy image of herself at the old ranch with Felipe and his father!

In her dream the old house was not in its present dilapidated condition, but had been made beautiful and luxurious following the plans which Felipe had more than once confided to her.

For always he talked of beautifying his old home and of his music and travel and of other delightful things, but never of war, or self-sacrifice, or hard work.

Felipe had not been informed whether his claim for exemption from war service had been accepted, and yet he seemed to regard the matter as settled.

So Gerry also forgot what was going on in the world about them, forgot what was being required of other young men, even though she had daily talks with the soldiers.

But at last the night for the public performance of "As You Like It" arrived.

The Camp Fire girls had not erred in their prediction that their guardian's reputation was sufficient to insure them a large audience. Mrs. Burton had secured the aid of a well-known California actor, Arthur Whitney, to play Orlando to her Rosalind. For the past two weeks he had been living in one of the hotels near the open-air theater, where he had many friends.

In the neighboring cities and towns the newspapers had devoted columns of unpaid advertising to notices of the play and the opportunity it afforded for seeing the famous American actress. Added to this was the fact that the proceeds from the performance were to be devoted to the recreation fund for the boys in the southern California cantonment.

Long before the night of the performance, every ticket of admission to the theater had been sold, and as much standing room as possible.

Fronting the entrance to the open-air theater stood three or four palm trees so trimmed as to give the effect of a green canopy.

Inside the theater were rows of rustic benches and in the foreground the open-air stage surrounded by a background of shrubs. Around the enclosure was a thick hedge.

Once inside the little theater and one was in so unique a setting, it was as if one were shut away in an enchanted world.

No more charming place could have been discovered for the performance of Shakespeare's comedy. The atmosphere and the scenery of the "Forest of Arden" were already secure.

A thrill of anticipation ran through the audience with the tinkling of a number of bells to announce the opening of the play.

Then the actors entered from behind a screen of shrubs to the left of the stage. The first conversation is between Orlando and old Adam.

The real interest of the audience waited, of course, upon the appearance of the star, and soon after Rosalind and Celia appeared on the lawn before the Duke's palace.

Mrs. Burton had played the character of Rosalind many times; the courage and gaiety of one of the most charming of all Shakespeare's heroines were essentially her own characteristics.

Tonight, on making her entrance, she had to pause for a moment to acknowledge the storm of applause. The first speech was Marta's, and Mrs. Burton was glad of the respite, remembering her own tragic first appearance and wondering if Marta could be suffering half so much.

Several times before the actual performance, she had been afraid that her solicitude for her amateur company would seriously interfere with her own acting.

Marta managed her first speech as Celia bravely. If one recalls her line, it is a brief one:

"I pray thee, Rosalind, sweet my coz, be merry."

Then Rosalind takes the center of the stage and while she is there, but few eyes are turned away from her. All the grace and charm of the one-time Polly O'Neill returned to the great actress in the hours when she was playing, and now added to her natural gifts were the long years of experience and training.

Tonight Mrs. Burton's voice charmed her audience with its peculiar magic, her every movement kept one fascinated.

Marta Clark too scored a distinct success as Celia. She had been awkward and self-conscious at rehearsals and no one had believed in her. But whether she needed the spur of the actual production, or had learned more than any one realized from playing with Mrs. Burton, certainly she showed unusual ease and pliancy for an amateur actress. More than once during the performance Mrs. Burton managed to whisper her congratulations, stirring Marta to fresh efforts.

Gerry did not do a great deal of acting, but as Phebe she was such a ravishingly pretty shepherdess that one thought of little else. Peggy's character study of Audrey, the country wench, showed such an amusing combination of stupidity and common sense that in spite of the unimportance of the part, she won a real triumph.

Lieutenant Carson at least presented a fine appearance as the melancholy Jaques.

The one failure among the company of youthful artists was Felipe Morris, upon whose natural ability Mrs. Burton and all the other players had depended.

It was surprising, for during all the rehearsals Felipe had always acted so agreeably that even the stage manager had only words of praise for him.

Yet the Touchstone who danced gracefully out before the footlights on the occasion of the real performance was a different Touchstone.

By a kind of natural instinct Mrs. Burton instantly recognized the fact. Even through his make-up and his motley costume of stripes and caps and bells, one could discern that Felipe's thoughts were not concentrated upon his performance.

Touchstone spoke his lines with the proper combination of drollery and impertinence, yet there was no suggestion of real wit or merriment. The very jangling of his bells was depressing.

Once in a hurried moment behind the scenes Mrs. Burton managed to inquire: "Is there anything the matter, Felipe? Are you not well?"

Felipe only laughed and shook his head. "What should be the matter? Am I falling down on my part? I shall try and brace up in the next act."

If Touchstone was a failure in his acting, Felipe sang as never before. It was not Gerry alone, listening behind the scenes, who was completely fascinated.

One of Touchstone's ballads is of the eternal romance of love and spring time. Felipe's voice held a freshness, a clear sweetness that went straight to the hearts of his audience.

"It was a lover and his lass,With a hey, and a ho, and a hey nonino,That o'er the green corn-field did passIn the spring time, the only pretty ring time,When birds do sing, hey ding a ding, ding;Sweet lovers love the spring."

The play was finally over, and if the curtain could not be rung down, at least the players bowed their thanks and farewells, standing together in a long line with Mrs. Burton in the center.

In order that they might avoid the confusion and fatigue of meeting so many strangers and receiving their congratulations after the play had ended, Mrs. Burton previously had invited her company of actors to motor over to Sunrise camp to a supper party as soon as they could slip away.

Gerry was returning in the motor with Mrs. Burton.

She chanced to be standing alone for a moment waiting for the others who were shaking hands with some new acquaintances, when Felipe Morris touched her upon the arm.

"Gerry, I must speak to you by yourself tonight after we reach the Sunrise camp. Please, no matter what happens, let nothing interfere with my seeing you. I have something to tell you and something to ask you which will affect all our future."

CHAPTER XV

"I WILL MARRY YOU, IF EVER I MARRY WOMAN"

To Gerry Williams it seemed as if their long supper party would never end.

The supper was served outdoors on a number of small tables. Through an accident Gerry was seated at so great a distance from Felipe that it was not possible to see his face and so guess from his expression something of what he desired to tell her.

Gerry was puzzled. If what he wished to say had to do with their future happiness, why had he looked so disturbed? And why should it be imperative that he make his confession tonight?

Already it was late, past midnight, and they were both weary. There would be tomorrow and other days.

Really she would have preferred not to talk with Felipe alone tonight. To slip away from the others would be difficult, and without Mrs. Burton's consent Gerry did not like the idea. Yet she did not dare ask for permission, being convinced that because of the lateness of the hour her request would be refused.

She felt that she must do what Felipe had begged of her. There had been something in his manner at once imperative and beseeching.

An unaccustomed shyness, almost a sense of fear, had seized upon Gerry; nevertheless she was prepared to follow Felipe's bidding, no matter how difficult.

To eat or talk gaily to the others was hard. In a half-hearted fashion, Gerry accomplished both results.

Immediately after the supper was finished the guests began saying their farewells.

The hour was long past the one when the young officers and soldiers were required to return to the cantonment. But owing to the play and Mrs. Burton's efforts in their behalf, they had received a special permit from the officer in command of their camp to remain away several hours later than their regulations demanded.

In the midst of the good-bys Gerry and Felipe moved swiftly toward each other.

"We must get away now, Felipe, while no one is thinking of us. I can only talk to you for a moment."

Even as she spoke Gerry was walking toward the beach with the young man following. In this way at least what they had to say to each other would not be overheard. There was no nearby place where they could actually escape observation.

In front of Sunrise camp the beach stretched long and level, broken only by small rocks, which afforded a shadow, not a shelter. Behind the little group of tents and Mrs. Burton's house were the level fields of a great ranch. There were no trees worthy of the name in sight.

"But I can't say what I must to you in one minute, Gerry. I must have time to explain many things. Surely you will go somewhere else with me. Here on the open beach we may be interrupted at any moment."

Gerry only moved on more rapidly. "I don't know where else to go, Felipe. We can walk along the beach until perhaps we are out of sight of the others. Then afterwards I can tell Mrs. Burton that we only intended taking a short walk."

"Very well," Felipe murmured, but Gerry could guess that he was annoyed.

"I suppose to a girl, Gerry, conventions are dearer than anything else in life. So since what I intend is to ask you to break one of them, perhaps I might as well not speak to you," he began, when they had nearly reached the water.

The ocean was not so calm as usual tonight on this particular line of coast. Great waves were rolling in, breaking and curling in white spirals of foam.

If there had been a storm, it was somewhere out in the ocean, for although there was no moon the stars were everywhere a shining glory.

"I don't know what you mean, Felipe," Gerry answered quietly.

She was still wearing her lovely shepherdess costume of pale blue and white, the pointed bodice and panniers of blue satin, the skirt and sleeves of muslin and lace. Mrs. Burton had insisted on Gerry's using a long white coat which was her property, so coming back in the motor she had slipped this on over her dress. Now the wind was blowing the coat open, revealing the soft comeliness of the satin and lace costume beneath.

Her shepherdess hat she had discarded and instead had tied a blue chiffon scarf around her hair.

Nevertheless, in spite of her frivolous and charming costume, Gerry Williams' expression was entirely serious.

"No, of course you do not understand. I am sorry," Felipe apologized. "You see, it has been such a horrible evening for me with all the foolishness of the play and my acting a clown's part, when I have been wishing every minute to get you away and tell you what has happened."

"But what has happened?" Gerry inquired anxiously and yet with patience.

"The exemption board has refused my claim. I only heard the pleasant news late this afternoon," Felipe answered.

Gerry's first sensation was one of intense personal sympathy.

Simply and naturally she slipped her hand inside Felipe's.

"I don't know what to say to you. I am so grieved for you. It is too dreadful, your being forced to join the army when you so hate the whole idea. Can't something more be done? Surely you and your father must have influence out here!"

Felipe shook his head. "Influence does not count; besides, if father has any influence he would not use it in my behalf, not in this connection. When I told him this afternoon what had occurred he merely said: 'I wish you had done your duty in the beginning, my son, without bringing the stigma of disgrace upon our name by trying to escape your responsibility. I did not suppose your claim for exemption would be considered, as your excuse was too flimsy.'"

For an instant Gerry hesitated, then she said, her voice shaking. "I do not mean to be rude, but I can not understand your father. You are his only son and are no relation to me, and yet it does not seem to me I can bear your going over to France, where you will be so unhappy, where you may be wounded. But I must not talk of these things. How soon must you begin your training, Felipe, and do you think you will be in a camp near your home?"

Until this instant Gerry had not considered herself, had not realized the failure of her dream. Now she had a little sinking sense of loneliness and disappointment. Nevertheless Felipe was still first in her thoughts.

"I wish I could do something to help you."

"You can, Gerry," Felipe returned, strengthening his hold on her hand. "I am not going to be drafted, Gerry. I am going over the border into Mexico tomorrow to remain until the war is over. I told you that I had no difficulty in being taken for a Mexican. I can speak the language and I don't look unlike one. This isn't an entirely new idea on my part, for I have been thinking and planning what I should do if my exemption claim were refused. I tell you I can not endure a soldier's existence, the dirt and the hard work and the discipline and then worse, blood and suffering and death. For even if all this does not come to me, I must see it. Oh, I know I am not a man, Gerry, and you probably despise me for feeling like this. But I can not help it. I was born for beauty and happiness, for music and — well, we are not all made alike."

"No, Felipe, I don't despise you; I think I understand," Gerry replied instantly. But there was no question with her of understanding. She was thinking of Felipe's happiness, of his safety. "Isn't it pretty dangerous what you are planning to do? If you are caught won't you be imprisoned?" she asked.

Felipe nodded. "Yes, but I am going to take the chance. It is worth the danger to me."

"You are intending to say good-by to me tonight then?" Gerry questioned. "I am glad you told me. No one in the world will ever be able to force your secret from me."

"Then you could be brave for my sake?" Felipe demanded.

But when Gerry did not answer, he began walking impatiently up and down within a few feet of her.

"I don't know what to say or do, Gerry," he continued after a moment. "I am not a rogue and I do not want to do you an injustice. But you told me once that you had no people of your own, that your father is dead and that your mother always has left you in common boarding houses, with no one to look after you, since you were a tiny girl. You told me that you had no real friend until Mrs. Burton took a fancy to you and has tried to give you some happiness. Now I can't bear the thought of your going so far away to live by yourself when I care for you so much. After tonight we may never even be able to see each other again in many years. Still I realize that you are very young, Gerry, and the fact that I am four or five years older makes the whole thing much more my responsibility than yours. Besides there is the danger of your crossing into Mexico with me and being forced to live there, one cannot say how long."

Gerry appeared utterly bewildered and unhappy. "But what do you mean, Felipe? I don't think I understand you."

"I mean I am asking you to marry me, Gerry." Felipe answered with an entire softening of his manner and expression. "But I realize I am asking you more than that, because I want you to marry me without telling any one and then slip over the border into Mexico with me to live until the war is past. If anything happens and I am caught, why, at least you will be safe, for my father will look after you. I did not want to ask you to marry me in this way, Gerry, I do not like the idea any more than you do. I had planned to tell you I cared for you and to tell Mrs. Burton also. I was even willing to wait for a year or more if you both thought it necessary. But now this difficulty of mine alters everything, and these are war times, when one is not expected to behave in an ordinary fashion."

In order to insure his own way, Felipe was in truth a good pleader. Besides, Gerry was already deeply under his influence.

Now Felipe's unexpected request made her both happy and unhappy, for she could not fail to be glad that he cared for her, although she knew she had no right to agree to his request.

The ethical side of the question of Felipe's intention to escape military service apparently made no impression upon Gerry one way or the other; the question seemed so entirely his to decide. Her feeling was merely that she could not bear to marry him and not tell even Mrs. Burton until afterwards.

If she were a little older she believed the situation would have appeared less formidable, then she would have had a clearer right to decide for herself. Under the circumstances she must not consider Felipe's suggestion even for a moment.

Yet she had only to answer, "No," and things would be as before.

For Felipe himself was uncertain and frightened of what he was asking. If he did not appreciate the full selfishness and wrong of it, nevertheless he did realize it in part. Gerry faced the alternative before replying. If she refused Felipe's offer, in a little while she must return to Chicago to take up her old existence in a common boarding house with nothing in her future except to learn to make her own living. But these things were no longer so important, the one important fact was that she might be losing Felipe forever.

Gerry cherished few illusions. If Felipe were successful in escaping military service they could not meet again until the war was over and in that time many changes would have occurred. Would Felipe remember her, or would he be less lonely in his self-imposed exile if she were to spend it with him? Whatever trouble she and Felipe might have to face, would she not prefer to face it with him rather than have him leave her alone?

"I cannot bear to deceive Mrs. Burton, Felipe. I owe her so much; she has been kinder than I have ever told you, kinder than perhaps you imagine. Besides, I care for her a great deal and I don't see how such a difficult idea as you have suggested can ever be arranged."

In Gerry's last words lay her confession. Felipe had triumphed. Had she tried she might have persuaded him to face his obligation, to make the sacrifice of himself which his country demanded. She was not equal to the test.

"But I do know how to manage," Felipe answered. "And I shall be very careful. I understand certain things better than you do. I have an old nurse who is married and lives not far away. She will come with us and stay with you until the ceremony is over. Afterwards she will return and explain what we have done to Mrs. Burton and my father. You can write and beg Mrs. Burton to forgive you; she will after a time, I am sure. We will be so happy, Gerry dear. I have plenty of money, as I drew all I possessed out of the bank this afternoon. I am sure it will last us for a time and then I can get hold of more."

The thing which Gerry and Felipe were planning to do was not only a foolish thing; it held dishonor and sorrow, and yet neither of them at the time seemed to appreciate this.

"Be ready the day after tomorrow, please, Gerry. I'll ask Mrs. Burton to allow you to go for a walk or a drive with me. I promise you there shall be no difficulties. But, quick, good-night; some one is coming."

Mrs. Burton herself was walking down the beach toward them. "Come, Gerry, please, it is time you were in bed. I was frightened when I found you were not with the other girls. Felipe, I don't think it quite fair of you to have kept Gerry away from us so long. Will you thank your father for the roses he sent me tonight?"

Felipe held out his hand.

"You are awfully kind, Mrs. Burton, and I do deserve a scolding. Gerry and I had not realized how long we had been talking, as there are so many things we like saying to each other. Will you forgive me and let me come back soon again?"

Mrs. Burton put her arm about Gerry.

"Not too soon, please, Felipe. Goodnight."

CHAPTER XVI
GERRY'S OPPORTUNITY

The next day, weary from the long strain of the rehearsals and the final production of their play, and feeling a comfortable sense of relaxation following a labor well accomplished, the Sunrise Camp Fire members spent an unusually quiet day.

Mrs. Burton remained in her little house resting and reading.

After accomplishing the necessary domestic tasks, Mrs. Webster and the girls sat about in little groups, knitting and talking over the unexpectedly brilliant success of their play.

Of the Camp Fire girls, Gerry Williams alone kept apart from the others for the greater part of the day. Now and then she would appear with her knitting and dropping down beside some one would remain for perhaps half an hour, but seldom longer. By the end of that time she seemed to grow restless and would start off on walks by herself, but never a great distance from camp. Once disappearing inside her sleeping tent, which was unoccupied, she stayed there alone for several hours.

No one paid any particular attention to Gerry or realized that she was in an unusual frame of mind. The Camp Fire girls had spent so many months together that they did not take one another's moods seriously; besides, Gerry was not an especial favorite or intimate with any one of the girls except Sally Ashton. And Sally frequently considered Gerry far too addicted to moods, which were disturbing to her own comfortable placidity.

Indeed, Gerry's only real friend in the Sunrise Camp Fire, the only person who in any way understood her temperament and the circumstances of her past sufficiently well to offer her real sympathy and affection, was Mrs. Burton.

On this same day it chanced that Dan Webster was away looking after a small business matter.

Billy was engaged with his labors at the war camp. But now that the play was over Mrs. Webster was beginning to concern herself more seriously with the behavior of her erratic son. Billy had taken advantage of the absorption of his family and friends to continue to pursue his own way in an even more determined and secretive fashion.

If Mrs. Burton had not spent the day inside her house, whether or not she would have observed Gerry's restlessness, her troubled expression, her moments of pallor and the swift flush succeeding them, no one can say.

Certainly all that day never for long did Gerry have Mrs. Burton out of her mind. First she would think of Felipe and what he had asked of her and then immediately after of Mrs. Burton's friendship and kindness.

The facts of Gerry's life were commonplace enough, but for that reason they seemed to Gerry the harder to endure.

Her mother and father had married when they were young and clerking together in a small village store. After Gerry's birth they conceived the idea of becoming traveling sales people.

When Gerry was a tiny child they tried taking her about with them, often leaving her alone for long, lonely hours in strange hotel rooms. After she grew older, arrangements were made for her to board in Chicago, the city her parents visited oftener than any other. But when Gerry was fourteen her father died and a year later her mother married a little town store keeper.

It was at this time Gerry Williams realized she would be forced to face the future for herself. It is true her mother and stepfather offered her a home with them and the opportunity to work in their shop. But Gerry had never cared for her mother and now hated her stepfather, while the thought of the little town store was abhorrent. Yet there was no particular reason for this attitude save that Gerry had always been antagonistic to her environment for as long as she could remember.

She was so utterly unlike her own people both in appearance, manner and nature that she was a puzzle to all of them. No one of them could have told from whom she inherited her delicate prettiness, her love of luxury and refinement.

One day, learning of Mrs. Burton's presence in Chicago, suddenly Gerry conceived the idea of going to her and applying for the position of maid. If she must work she thought that she would like better than most things to live with a famous woman and perhaps travel with her and see something of the world.

At the moment of Gerry's arrival it chanced that by accident Mrs. Burton was at home and free from other engagements, so she decided to see and talk to her. Naturally Gerry was too young and untrained for the position she desired; moreover, Mrs. Burton had no need for the services of a maid, since Marie had been living with her a number of years. But she grew interested in her pretty guest, and feeling the need of sympathy, Gerry was glad to pour forth her story.

Ever after this visit, although no member of her family aside from her husband had been informed of the fact, Mrs. Burton had been paying Gerry's board in Chicago during the winters, only urging her to try to educate herself for some work in the future. For several summers, as we know, Gerry had been invited to be a member of the Sunrise Camp Fire group.

Therefore in a measure Gerry realized how poor a return she would be offering should she slip away with Felipe without confessing her intention to Mrs. Burton.

Not once, but perhaps a dozen times, her mind was almost made up to find Mrs. Burton and tell her everything. For Gerry believed that by some method she could induce her friend to understand how deeply she cared for Felipe. There would be the argument of youth against their immediate marriage; but youth is not always only a question of the number of years one has lived, and Gerry felt convinced that she suddenly had grown old.

Nevertheless there was always this stumbling block. How could she acknowledge her own intention and Felipe's without betraying Felipe's secret? To divulge the fact that he was planning to escape military service by crossing over the border into Mexico and hiding there was out of the question.

Undoubtedly Gerry should have more fully appreciated the enormity of Felipe's purpose, his selfishness and disloyalty. Strange that she should expect to find happiness with a man who wished to begin their life together by an act of deception and cowardice! Nevertheless, by this time one must have learned to understand Gerry's disposition sufficiently well to accept the fact that she did not fully understand, so completely was she under Felipe's influence. Yet Felipe must not be allowed to bear the entire burden of their wrong doing. Certainly Gerry was not marrying Felipe for his sake only, but also for the happiness and the ease which she believed the future would insure her.

Notwithstanding this, since life is seldom guided by one clear motive, but by many mixed ones, Gerry was also ardently and sincerely in love.

Her failure to grasp the extent of the danger she and Felipe were facing and the possible injury to her own reputation was due to three causes. The first of these was sheer stupidity, the second an actual lack of education and the third Gerry's conviction that this was her solitary chance for saving Felipe from the difficulties and dangers of a soldier's life and at the same time securing him for herself.

In the end, as one might have guessed, Gerry Williams made no confession.

Instead, in the hours when she had remained alone in her sleeping tent, she had packed a few possessions in her satchel, hiding the bag under her bed and wondering at the same time how she would ever manage to get it away the next day without exciting comment.

The next day Fortune appeared to favor Gerry, as the fickle Dame does now and then, when one had best be thwarted.

Immediately after their luncheon the Camp Fire girls decided to go upon a long walk. So much time had been given to the rehearsals of "As You Like It" that they had been exercising far less than usual in the past weeks.

The wool for knitting and materials for making bandages having recently given out, Mrs. Webster offered to go into town with Dan to buy whatever was required.

So, through a combination of quite ordinary circumstances, Sunrise camp was deserted except by Mrs. Burton, Marie and Gerry.

Mrs. Burton did not feel equal to the long hike and Gerry simply declined without giving a reason.

Since her farewell to Felipe about thirty hours before, she had received no word from him and yet this afternoon Gerry knew he would appear. Now and then she even hoped he would not come, at least not until the next day, or even the one after that.

Soon after the other girls departed, Mrs. Burton asked Gerry to sit beside her and talk while she rested in the sunshine.

A small fire was always kept burning at Sunrise camp, no matter how warm the day, for the small amount of heat made no appreciable difference and the fire was always being needed for cooking.

So Marie arranged an Indian blanket upon the ground away from the windward side of the fire and then went into her tent to write letters.

Afterwards Mrs. Burton lay down in such a position that she could look closely at Gerry.

In the few minutes they had been together without the others, she had noticed that Gerry looked pale and depressed.

"You are not worrying over anything, Gerry?" Mrs. Burton asked.

Gerry shook her head. "Certainly not. What have I to worry about—except everything?"

Perhaps it was unfortunate that Mrs. Burton chose this time to talk to Gerry about her future, although, since her mind really was made up, probably nothing would have altered her decision.

"I don't want to worry you, or to have you worry, dear," Mrs. Burton began, "but I do wish it were possible for you to find some occupation that would interest you. It would make you ever so much happier! Forgive me if I have seen that you are more restless, less content than the other Camp Fire girls. And whatever work you wish to do, I do not wish you to go into it unprepared, a woman needs more training these days to make a success than a man. It has meant so much to me to give my time and energy to the art I love. I want you to have the same luck, Gerry."

Then Mrs. Burton reached out her hand, but her companion did not seem to observe it.

"I am sorry, I know I am a disappointment," she answered. "But the trouble with me is that I am stupid and no work of any character interests me. I might as well tell you the truth."

For a moment Mrs. Burton did not reply. Gerry's answer had made her impatient, and for this reason she felt it best not to argue.

"Very well, perhaps the interest will come later. You are young enough to wait, Gerry, and please do not think I am not more than anxious to help you. You know it is only on your account I worry. I so wish the circumstances of your life were happier, my dear. I hate your being lonely."

Then as Gerry's eyes were filling with tears and when she was having a struggle not to break down entirely and make her confession, she and Mrs. Burton both heard at the same instant a gay voice singing as it approached nearer to them:

"It was a lover and his lass,With a hey, and a ho, and a hey nonino."

"Here comes Touchstone, Gerry! What a charming voice Felipe has! I know you must feel relieved to be released from such a prosy talk as we were having."

If Felipe had not been a particularly successful actor at the production of their play, Gerry was amazed by his present acting.

He had suggested that they were either to motor or to drive away from Sunrise camp. Now he appeared on foot in the most casual fashion with his guitar swung over his shoulder.

After bowing politely to Gerry, he immediately dropped down upon the ground beside Mrs. Burton and finished his song:

"And therefore take the present time,With a hey, and a ho, and a hey nonino;For love is crowned with the primeIn springtime...."

Nor did Felipe rise, or ask that Gerry be allowed to walk with him after his song was concluded. He merely continued talking in a casual fashion with Mrs. Burton.

In half an hour, having finished their errands unexpectedly early, Mrs. Webster and Dan returned to camp. Dan went away immediately to put up the car and Mrs. Burton arose to go indoors with her sister.

Not until then did Felipe ask that Gerry be allowed to walk with him. He made the request with apparent indifference.

Mrs. Burton hesitated.

"Gerry thought she was too tired to walk with the girls! But never mind. If you won't go very far or stay too long, I suppose I must pay my actors in some fashion for their services, and I have had no opportunity to thank you."

Then, as she moved away, she called back:

"Don't forget to take your coat or a sweater with you, Gerry; it may turn unexpectedly cool."

So Gerry, feeling that her face was flushing crimson and her hands becoming like ice, was able to disappear inside her tent at the moment she desired.

When she came out with her satchel the coat was hanging over it; besides, there was no one in sight to observe her own and Felipe's departure.

But the moment they started Felipe said quickly:

"Don't be worried, Gerry darling. I have a motor waiting for us about a mile away and my old nurse is there to take care of you. Her husband is with her and they are perfectly respectable and devoted to me. They will come back as soon as we are safely married and let Mrs. Burton and father know. They can't tell them where we have gone, of course. They can simply say we have gone on a honeymoon. It will be all right. Lots of people run away and are married; it saves such a lot of fuss for one thing. Later on, if you like, we can write where we are, because neither Mrs. Burton nor father would betray us. I want, if possible, to cross over the border into Mexico tonight at dusk."

The rest of the afternoon passed like a strange and not a happy dream to Gerry.

But whatever arrangements were necessary, whatever the law required of them, Felipe seemed to have managed all the formalities. As they drove from one place to another Gerry sat in the back of the automobile next to Felipe's old nurse, not even making an effort to talk to her and saying nothing to Felipe. Now and then Felipe made little anxious inquiries to find out if she were all right and Gerry only nodded her head in reply.

In the house of a clergyman in a small town not many miles away the ceremony was finally performed. Gerry declared that her parents had given their consent, knowing well enough they would be delighted to hear of her marriage. Felipe Morris was of course several years more than the legal age. Besides Felipe's nurse and her husband the wife and daughter of the clergyman also appeared as witnesses.

But when the moment came for parting with their companions, Gerry begged that she be allowed to write a note to Mrs. Burton. The note was very short; Gerry scarcely understood what she was writing, nevertheless it said a great deal:

"DEAR MRS. BURTON:

"You will never be able to forgive me and I know I do not deserve that you should. Only pray I may be happy, because now the wedding ceremony is over and Felipe Morris and I are married, I am dreadfully frightened.

"Yours with all love,

"GERRY."

The rest of the late afternoon was even more like a strange dream.

At the border between Mexico and the United States Felipe managed successfully to deceive the guard. He had changed his costume and wore a Mexican one, he spoke Spanish and gave a name which was not his own. Gerry, who was wearing a veil tied closely about her head, the guard scarcely noticed.

Felipe explained that he and his wife had driven over into California earlier in the day and were now on their way back to their home in Mexico. By a stroke of good fortune the guard had only been on duty a few hours, having changed places with another soldier. Therefore he had no way of disproving Felipe's story; moreover, he happened to be new to his work.

Never so long as she lived was Gerry to forget her first sight of the strange desert land of Mexico, which she saw when dusk was falling.

The earth was a sea of sand with funny little hut-like houses sprinkled here and there, hung with gay signs written in a language Gerry did not comprehend. Beyond them was a fringe of high bare hills, now purple in the evening shadows.

Suddenly she realized her own and Felipe's exile. They were without home or country; worse, they were deserters.

For fear he was suffering an even deeper regret and remorse than had laid hold upon her, Gerry dared not look or speak to Felipe as their car carried them further and further away from their friends.

CHAPTER XVII

FOLLY AND COURAGE

Before information of any kind concerning her mysterious disappearance was received from Gerry Williams, every member of the Sunrise Camp Fire had become alarmed. But it must be confessed that the girls were more annoyed than they were agitated.

Mrs. Burton and Mrs. Webster were necessarily anxious, yet as Mrs. Webster had never felt an especial interest or affection for Gerry, she was less so than her sister.

The Camp Fire girls had returned from their walk in time for a late afternoon tea. They were just finishing when Marta Clark inquired what had become of Gerry, and why she was not having tea with them?

Then for the first time Mrs. Burton mentioned that Gerry had gone away from camp with Felipe Morris several hours before. But as she had promised to return in a short time, already she was beginning to feel worried for fear something had happened.

Then another hour went by and the dusk began to descend. But since it was late summer and the days were long, some time would still elapse before actual darkness.

Nevertheless Mrs. Burton at first betrayed her nervousness by walking alone up and down the little traveled road beyond the camp. Finally she came back to the group of girls, who were still loitering about their camp fire before clearing away the tea things.

"Do be good to me, Peggy. I know you are already tired from your long walk and I won't go far," she promised. "But somehow I am so uncomfortable about Gerry I cannot keep still. I know I am absurd, but I have one of those ridiculous premonitions which never amount to anything. If she does not come back in another hour, I shall motor over to the ranch to inquire if Mr. Morris has received any word from Felipe."

In spite of the fact that Peggy was tired and also annoyed at what she presumed to be Gerry's selfish unconcern, she got up instantly at Mrs. Burton's request, and as they started off on their walk placed her arm affectionately inside her aunt's.

"I don't see why you allow yourself to become so worked up over Gerry's staying away from camp with Felipe longer than you approve," said Peggy with her usual directness. "If you do not realize how much she is interested in him, you are the only one of us who is blind. Gerry has not cared for anything except her friendship with Felipe all this summer. She has an affection for you, but except for you everything in our Camp Fire life has bored her."

Knowing by her aunt's expression that she was annoyed by her critical attitude, nevertheless Peggy, who was not in a good humor, went on with her plain speaking.

"Sometimes I have thought Gerry was really in love with Felipe; at other times I have simply thought she liked him just because he was a man and showed her some attention. Gerry is the type of girl who has not the faintest interest in other girls."

"Is this your opinion alone, or the opinion of all the Camp Fire girls?" Mrs. Burton inquired in a tone it was difficult to translate.

Peggy flushed. "Perhaps it is my opinion alone, since it sounds rather hateful. In any case, I have no right to speak except for myself. But if you wish to know the truth, the opinion is pretty general."

"Have the girls the same attitude toward you, Peggy, because of your interest in Ralph Marshall?" Mrs. Burton demanded. "You know how much of your time and thought you give to him these days, even though you rarely mention his name, and you have many more people to care for than Gerry, who is rather singularly alone. If you girls are not fond of her I am not surprised that she prefers Felipe Morris, who, after all, is exceptionally attractive."

Peggy was suddenly upon the defensive.

"I don't think I have allowed my interest in Ralph to interfere with my friendships with the Camp Fire girls," she argued defensively. "But I did not intend being disagreeable about Gerry. She is always amiable and sweet, only it is difficult not to resent her indifference and her absorption in herself."

After this speech Mrs. Burton and Peggy continued their walk in silence for a few moments. Then Mrs. Burton said in a different tone:

"When Gerry comes back this evening, Peggy, I wish you would try to be particularly nice to her. If she has become too much interested in Felipe I cannot help being sorry for her. I have never told you girls much of Gerry's history because she preferred my not telling. But she has had a hard time and no one has ever really cared for her. Her father is dead and her mother an impossibly common person without any good traits of character, so far as I have been able to discover, which would redeem her commonness. So things will be all the more difficult for Gerry if she is under the impression she cares for Felipe. In a little time our Camp Fire summer will be over and they will be separated."

Peggy nodded. "I will do my best. I am sorry to have been so critical. At least Gerry does not make disagreeable speeches about other people! But you are mistaken if you think any of us has ever been unkind to her; it is only that we have found it impossible to become intimate. Of course she and Sally like each other. But if there are facts in Gerry's life she does not wish to discuss, I can understand why she prefers not to develop too close an intimacy with the rest of us, who know almost everything about one another. But don't worry, I presume some accident has delayed Gerry and Felipe. Suppose we return to camp? They may have taken some other route and arrived by this time."

But of course Gerry was not at the Sunrise camp. Within five minutes after Mrs. Burton's and Peggy's return, an automobile appeared containing an unknown man and woman.

The woman asked to be permitted to speak to Mrs. Burton alone.

Then, as she stood hesitating, trying to make up her mind what to say first, suddenly she remembered Gerry's crumpled little note.

For Gerry's sake it was as well that the news of her runaway marriage was imparted to her Camp Fire guardian and friend in this fashion, for the note revealed infinitely more than Gerry realized. With Mrs. Burton's understanding of human nature she understood something of the struggle, something of the temptation to which Gerry had yielded. Therefore in the midst of her surprise and anger she could not forget the note's final pathetic appeal.

Neither the woman nor man would tell much more than the bare facts of Gerry's and Felipe's marriage. They insisted that the ceremony was entirely legal and that immediately afterwards the young couple had gone away. In truth, they could not tell more, since as a matter of precaution Felipe had not informed either his nurse or her husband of his plans.

After appreciating that the marriage had become a reality and that there was nothing she could do or say which would make any difference, Mrs. Burton asked but few questions. She knew that Felipe's father would come to her as soon as he learned what had taken place and she preferred to discuss the situation with him and not with strangers.

Of necessity it was Mrs. Burton who imparted the information to the Camp Fire girls, but she merely told what she knew as briefly as possible, adding no comment. Then she went away to be alone. She was not thinking of Gerry's ingratitude, of the poor return she had made for her interest and assistance, but she was thinking of Gerry herself. Gerry was so young and she and Felipe knew each other so slightly. Then, as Mrs. Burton knew nothing at present of Felipe's attempt to hide in Mexico, it also occurred to her that he might soon be forced to join the army.

Left to themselves, the Camp Fire girls were not so lenient in their condemnation. It was Alice Ashton who chanced to voice the general sentiment.

"I cannot understand how any human being could behave as Gerry has done! Certainly she has proved how little the Camp Fire influence has meant to her! But there is no point in our criticising her, because some day Gerry will have to pay dearly enough."

CHAPTER XVIII

THE SUMMONS

Later in the same night, being unable to sleep, Mrs. Burton was aroused by hearing the approach of another motor car. It must have been between two and three o'clock in the dark hours before dawn when the earth is so strangely quiet. Moreover, cars were not in the habit of passing Sunrise camp at any hour, as it was too far from the main road to allure travelers.

Mrs. Burton quietly slipped on her dressing gown and slippers in order not to disturb her sister, who slept in the room with her. As she walked to the front door she was under the impression that Gerry must have returned home to camp and would wish to see her.

But outside it was so dark that for a moment she could see nothing. Then at a little distance off she discovered two figures standing close together. As Mrs. Burton drew nearer she recognized one of them as Dan Webster, and as Dan was fully dressed he could not have been in bed during the night. The other man was Lieutenant Carson.

"Yes, I have been worried all night," she overheard Dan say. "I persuaded mother to go to bed fairly early by telling her I would wait for Billy. But after midnight when he did not come I have not known what to do. I had no idea where to go to look for him. I was afraid something had happened. Is the accident serious?"

"If it were not I would never have wakened you at such an hour," Lieutenant Carson answered. "Please break the news to your mother and sister as quickly as you can and ask them to hurry. I brought over one of our army cars, so there need be no delay. On the way to camp I will tell you as much as I know."

Then Mrs. Burton stepped out of the shadow.

"Billy is hurt," she began, not asking a question, but stating a conviction. "What has he done?" she hesitated, her voice breaking.

"He has done something so wonderful there is not a soldier in camp who would not be proud to accomplish one-half so much. But he has been injured and — — " Lieutenant Carson tried to keep his own tones from becoming husky.

"I'll see your mother, Dan," said Mrs. Burton. "Will you please waken Vera and Peggy? If Billy is conscious when we arrive he will wish to have Vera near him."

Within ten minutes the four women and Dan were on their way with Lieutenant Carson to the army cantonment.

The lieutenant had asked Dan to drive the car during the first part of the journey so that he might explain what had occurred.

"Yes, Mrs. Webster, your son is in our Red Cross hospital and everything possible is being done for him. A doctor reached him almost at once. But I wish I could tell you exactly what happened. As it is I can only repeat the story the little chap told himself. No one knows anything else, but he has been perfectly conscious all along and I am told is not suffering a great deal," Lieutenant Carson faltered, wishing that the task in which he was engaged had fallen to some one else.

"Please tell us everything you can," Peggy urged. "I feel my mother had best know the truth before we reach Billy."

"As far as I could find out there have been two laborers employed at our camp who are traitors. In spite of all the official red tape and investigations, your son Billy seems to have been the only person who discovered the fact. The little fellow apparently called himself a pacifist and made friends with the men. Anyhow they must have believed he sympathized with them, for he has been watching them for some time. I don't know how long, I am having to guess a part of this. But they must have finally decided he was one of them, as they allowed him to find out their secrets. It is amazing. I don't see how he managed!"

"But you have not yet told us how Billy chanced to be at your camp tonight and how he came to be hurt, Lieutenant Carson," Peggy pleaded, knowing that the same thought was in all their minds.

"Billy knew there was mischief brewing without knowing exactly what the ruffians were planning to do, at least, that is the way I understand the facts," the young officer continued. "But it seems that when he had followed them to their meeting place earlier in the evening, he found out they had placed a bomb in one of our big buildings at camp which was set to go off at a certain hour tonight. Billy says he made the men believe he considered this a great idea, otherwise they would never have allowed him to escape. He seems to have had the nerve to get up and spout a little speech on pacifism before about half a dozen of them. I believe he said that if only the men managed to destroy our war camps, the United States would never be able to enter the war in Europe and so peace would soon have to be declared as the Allies couldn't go on without America's aid. Anyhow, after a while they let the little fellow go and he pretended to be starting for home. But instead he made for our camp.

"Perhaps he could have managed better. What I should have done in his place I don't know; but he was a little chap up against a pretty big proposition. He did not know how to get the news to camp unless he told some one out here what was about to take place. He was trying to slip into camp with his news when one of our sentries shot him. He was just able to tell the soldier who picked him up what his business was and—well, we found the infernal machine where he told us to look for it. And God only knows how many lives Billy has saved!"

"But my son will live?" Mrs. Webster inquired, with the quiet fortitude which comes now and then to some of us in the really great moments of our lives.

"I don't know, Mrs. Webster," Lieutenant Carson answered honestly. "I was only ordered to bring you to camp as quickly as possible."

Then the young officer took charge of the car, as he was more familiar with the road than Dan.

The southern dawn which Billy had learned to love in these past weeks was breaking into pale lavender and rose when the army automobile arrived at camp.

A good many of the soldiers were walking about, not caring to go back to sleep after what had occurred. More of them than one would imagine remembered seeing Billy about camp in the past few weeks, the delicate young fellow with the extraordinary blue eyes. Lucky thing for them that he had been around, but hard on him!

Captain Mason and Major Anderson, two of the officers who were friends of Mrs. Burton's, came forward to meet her and Mrs. Webster.

They led the way to the hospital, with the girls and Dan and Lieutenant Carson following.

"Your son has been asking for you, Mrs. Webster, only he said you were not to be frightened about him and we were not to let you know what had happened until breakfast time," Major Anderson remarked with that same huskiness in his voice which Lieutenant Carson had been unable to conceal. "This war has made many heroes and will make many more, but I don't know of a finer thing than your son has done. He must have known the risk he ran when he came out here alone tonight on such an errand."

At the door of the hospital, which was only a wooden house with a Red Cross flag outside, the doctor met the little company.

"You will be as quiet as you can and try not to excite him," he said, and there was something in his voice which made all questioning impossible.

Then Mrs. Webster and Dan and Peggy went inside the little hospital. Within a few moments Dan came out again with his head bowed and went away by himself without speaking.

"Will it be many hours, Doctor?" Mrs. Burton inquired.

The doctor shook his head.

"Not many."

Mrs. Burton was standing with her arm about Vera Lagerloff, feeling Vera's grief almost as deeply as her own. Without a tie of blood, without the right to be near him which his family had, Vera was yet closer to Billy in many ways than any other human being in the world.

"You shall see him soon, dear," Mrs. Burton murmured.

Vera nodded.

"Billy will send for me; there will be so many things he will wish to say," she replied and her tone was one of love and understanding.

"I don't think I can get on without Billy afterwards, Mrs. Burton. No one else has realized how wonderful he was, what beautiful things he was planning to do with his life." Vera was shivering so Mrs. Burton could only hold her more closely.

"I know, dear, and yet how could one do more than Billy has done? Greater love hath no man than this that he lay down his life for his friend. Billy's friends, remember, were never merely the few people he knew; his idea of friendship was a bigger thing than ours."

"Billy wishes to speak to you, Tante, and to Vera," Peggy said at this instant appearing at the open door. "Don't be unhappy at seeing him. He is not frightened and yet he understands perfectly he has only a little while."

Billy was lying on a cot with a nurse on one side of him and his mother on the other, but, except for this, looking much as he usually did.

His face was paler and the blue eyes even wider open, yet for once in his life they seemed to have lost their questioning look.

"I promised you not to get into mischief, Tante. Well, this is the last time; at least, I suppose it is my last. But after all one does not know; there may be other chances over there."

Billy was trying to smile and Mrs. Burton leaned over and kissed him.

"I know there will be, Billy, and you will take them as gallantly as you have done this one. Don't worry, old chap, I'll look after your mother and Peggy."

Then she turned away.

Vera had kneeled down and was hiding her face in the bed clothes.

It was to her Billy turned like a little boy.

"Please look at me, Vera, and tell me you are sorry. It was like me to do the right thing in the wrong way, wasn't it? Yet there are so many things I want to say, want to explain to people. You see it is all a question of our learning to understand each other better to end fighting and all the rest of it. You believed in me, didn't you, Vera? Yet you understand that I could not let the soldiers out here be killed when they are getting ready to give their lives for ours. What is that we read about Christ the other day, Vera?"

Vera held Billy's two hands folded closely in her own.

"Listen, dear, and remember this:

"'Christ is courage, Christ is adventure, he fights for us and with us against death.'"

CHAPTER XIX

PLANS FOR THE FUTURE

In a large hotel sitting-room a number of girls were grouped in various attitudes, discussing a question which evidently interested them.

"Does any one know why we are not to start east tomorrow as we planned?" Marta Clark inquired, glancing up from a city map which she had been studying.

"Why, no, not exactly," Bettina Graham answered her. "Tante did not tell us definitely. She merely said that something had occurred which made her feel it would be wiser for her to remain in California a few days longer, unless we were compelled to leave for home at once. Personally I cannot imagine what is keeping her here, as I know she is anxious to go home, now that our Camp Fire summer is over and Peggy and Aunt Mollie and Dan Webster have gone. I think it was wonderfully good of her to continue with our camping party after Billy's death, when she must have wished to leave with the others."

"I think I know why she seemed to change her mind so unexpectedly yesterday and canceled all our reservations for berths," Sally Ashton announced in the mysterious manner which Sally often assumed to the annoyance of the other girls. Since her arrival in the city, Sally temporarily had forsworn her war and Camp Fire abstinence and was at this moment engaged in eating chocolates which had just arrived by parcel post from Merton Anderson.

"How absurd you are, Sally! You know no more than the rest of us!" Alice Ashton argued with sisterly frankness.

Instead of replying, sanctimoniously tightening her lips, Sally added nothing to her original statement.

"Nevertheless, won't you please tell us what you think, Sally?" Vera Lagerloff requested, and because it was Vera who made the request Sally agreed.

Since Billy's death the Camp Fire girls had been as unobtrusively kind to Vera as they knew how to be. In a measure they appreciated what his loss must mean to her, although it was out of the question that they could fully understand the extent of Vera's loneliness, the feeling of emptiness which the future now seemed to offer her.

Vera's long and devoted friendship with Billy had separated her from the usual intimacy with other girls, nevertheless she was a general favorite. For a good many years Billy had required whatever time and thought she could spare from her ordinary duties and affections.

"I think, Vera, that Tante recently has heard some unexpected news of Gerry," Sally finally announced with the proper degree of solemnity and with a due sense of dramatic values.

At least she was a dramatic success to the extent of surprising her audience.

"What authority have you for such a statement, Sally?" Alice Ashton demanded in the superior voice and manner which Alice now and then affected.

Sally shrugged her shoulders. "I haven't any authority, I have a 'hunch'," she returned, appreciating how painfully her slang would annoy her intellectual sister.

"But how is it possible that Gerry could have written? Don't you think she and Felipe are still hiding in Mexico? We know that much from what Mr. Morris has told us! If Gerry should write to Mrs. Burton she might betray her own and Felipe's secret and she would not do that," Marta Clark protested.

"I did not say Gerry had written, I only said that I believed Tante had received some information concerning her," Sally answered, undisturbed by criticism.

In response to this speech the expressions on the faces of the four other girls became curiously alike.

125

"I don't believe if I were Mrs. Burton I should ever take an interest in Gerry again," Marta Clark announced. "Perhaps I am more in a position to say this than any of the rest of you, because all of you have some past association with Mrs. Burton; she was an intimate friend of your mothers. She simply chose to be kind to me and to invite me to spend this summer with her Camp Fire group without any especial reason, just as she has been good to Gerry. If I should repay her kindness as Gerry has done, I should never dare make the effort to see her again, or to ask her forgiveness, no matter how greatly I might desire it."

"I feel just as you do, Marta," Bettina Graham agreed.

But Sally gave a little protesting cough, holding a chocolate drop suspended in the air for an instant.

"Judge not, lest ye be judged," she declared sententiously, and then with a somewhat less self-righteous expression, "Was that quotation from the Bible or Shakespeare and did I quote correctly? The truth is I wish that all of you would not be so hard upon Gerry. I know you think it silly and impossible for a girl not yet eighteen to be really in love, but just the same Gerry is in love with Felipe. As she is in love with him and he has been a coward and is now a fugitive from his own country, I don't suppose Gerry is so happy that all of you need be disagreeable about her. Personally I am perfectly sure that if Gerry wishes Tante's sympathy and help again, Tante would be sure to do whatever she could to help her."

"Hats off to Sally!" Bettina Graham remarked and no one disputed the suggestion. "Still of course, Sally dear, it is impossible that any news could have been received from Gerry, since she and Felipe must remain out of the country until the war is over and the whole circumstance of Felipe is forgotten," Bettina continued. "But suppose when Tante returns we inquire why we are to wait over in Los Angeles a few days more? I presume she would not object to explaining. I believe no one asked her the direct question."

"Yes, but she would have volunteered to tell had she wished us to know," Alice Ashton argued.

Vera Lagerloff, who had been sitting by an open window looking out toward a circle of hills which were like giant amethysts in the afternoon light, turned toward the other girls.

"Suppose if we have no other plans we spend tomorrow on Mount Lowe and give Mrs. Burton the opportunity to be alone," she suggested. "We have been at the seashore so long I am anxious for a day among the hills."

Then she addressed Marta Clark.

"You are mistaken, Marta, if you think all of us here, aside from you, have some past association with Mrs. Burton. I have none except that Billy and I always have been friends and he asked his aunt to take an interest in me. Now Mrs. Burton is going to do something for me which seems more wonderful than anything she has ever done for any one else, although I know she has been a fairy godmother to a good many people. But she is to pay my expenses and allow me to go to France to work in the devastated country which has lately been cleared of the Germans. 'The Field of Honor' is the name for this part of France which I like best. I hope to work among the homeless children. But in any case I have been brought up on a farm and can do farming work, which I have heard is especially needed. I am to study in New York City before I sail. Courses of study are being given there under the auspices of the French Huguenot societies."

An unusual silence followed Vera's long speech and then it was Sally Ashton who spoke first.

"For your sake, Vera, I am so glad, for I know the new life and the new work will mean a great deal to you just now. I only wish I were going with you."

"But you, Sally, what on earth could you do that would be useful in France?" Alice remonstrated, not because she wished to be disagreeable but to relieve the little tension which Vera's confidence had wrought.

"At least I can cook, which is a more useful accomplishment than any you can offer, Alice," Sally returned with such ridiculous spitefulness that the other girls laughed.

"I believe I am also envious of you, Vera," Bettina remarked. "All summer I have been feeling that we were not doing enough to help with the war merely by economizing and sewing and knitting, all the hundred and one small things we have tried to do. If we were boys we would be going through at least a little military training and in a few years would be able to volunteer. It is simply amazing what the girls and women are doing in England. So far we have not nearly approached their efforts. Do you know there is a 'Woman's Army Auxiliary Corps' already in France working directly behind the lines. I believe the Tommies call them 'The Tommy-waacs.' We have been talking about being behind the lines this summer, but I wish we could be more directly there."

"But what is the exact work the English girls are doing?" Alice demanded, as if she were seriously weighing a problem in her mind. "I am sure we can do the same things if they become necessary."

"I don't know all the varieties of war work of course, Alice," Bettina returned. "In Great Britain women and girls have taken the places of the men in more departments of labor than we can imagine. Of course we know they are working in munition shops and aeroplane factories and in ship building, and are telephone and telegraph operators. Now they are also working among the blind, being specially trained for the work, of course, and are actually driving ambulances and motor trucks near the fighting line. But I will bore you if I go on enumerating even the little I know. Personally I agree with, Vera, I should prefer to work among the children. Madame Montessori, the great Italian teacher, has been in the United States this summer trying to establish what she calls the order of the 'White Cross.' The members of the White Cross are to devote themselves to the care of the children who have suffered from the war. She says there is no hope of their growing into healthy and normal men and women unless they receive special care."

"Is there an organization anything like our own Camp Fire girls in France?" Sally Ashton demanded unexpectedly. "I know there is in England where they call themselves the 'Girl Scouts.' But I should think that young girls living and working together in France as we have been trying to do, might help each other and be useful to other people as well."

"I quite agree with you, Sally," Bettina returned. "Odd, that no one of us can answer your question! But as soon as we return East I mean to make it my business to find out if there is a French Camp Fire. At least we could write to the French Camp Fire girls if they exist."

At this instant the girls' conversation was interrupted by the sudden opening of a door and Mrs. Burton's entrance.

She was not in mourning but was wearing a black dress and hat which were unbecoming and made her look older.

"Why is everybody so serious?" she instantly demanded.

Before any one else could reply Sally Ashton answered:

"We are serious because we are thinking that some day we may ask you to take us to France to form Camp Fire clubs over there and to do whatever we can to help. Oh, of course I know we must learn more of what will be required of us and be prepared to make all kinds of sacrifices."

Flinging her hat on the bed with as great carelessness as if she were a girl and also as if she were pleased to be rid of it, Mrs. Burton replied:

"You are an amazing child, Sally. Even if I had the courage for such an undertaking, which I have not, do you suppose I would have sufficient influence with the parents of any one of you to persuade them to allow you to stir one foot away from your own land at a time like this? But I understand you have been hearing Vera's news. The circumstances with

Vera are exceptional. Wait here another moment, there is something I have to tell you."

Then Mrs. Burton disappeared into her bedroom which adjoined their hotel sitting-room. Their hotel was not in the center of the city but in a suburb a few miles out.

A few moments later she returned wearing a lavender crepe dressing gown and looking younger and more attractive.

For some reason she sat down next to Sally and put her arm about Sally's shoulders.

"I hope my information may interest you," she began with a slight suggestion of appeal in her voice, glancing from one of the girls to the other.

"Two days ago I received a letter from Mr. Morris telling me that Felipe had been arrested by the United States authorities. He had crossed over into California for the day in order to attend to some private business. I believe he wished to get some money from his father. He trusted, of course, in not being discovered, but was arrested within an hour."

"I suppose I ought to say I am sorry, if that is what you wish, Tante? But really I cannot. It seems to me exactly the fate that Felipe Morris deserves," Bettina Graham answered coldly.

"What will be done to Felipe as a punishment for having tried to escape the draft?" asked Alice Ashton. "I believe the punishment is very severe, is it not?"

"His father is afraid he will receive three years' imprisonment," Mrs. Burton replied without comment.

Then she heard a little horrified exclamation from the girl nearest her and Sally's face had whitened and her expression changed.

"But Gerry! What is to become of Gerry?" she demanded. "I know that she behaved very badly and that she ought to have persuaded Felipe to do his duty, instead of helping him to run away from it. But Gerry was dreadfully under Felipe's influence, and, anyhow, I don't care, I am terribly sorry for her," Sally ended incoherently, hiding her brown eyes behind her hand.

"I also am very sorry, Sally," Mrs. Burton added. "The fact of having done a wrong has never yet made any human being's punishment easier to bear. But I can tell you one thing about Gerry, Sally dear, since you alone seem interested. She is in California and is coming to see me tomorrow. She returned to California as soon as she received word of Felipe's arrest. She has been with Mr. Morris, and they of course will do whatever is in their power to have Felipe's sentence made as light as possible. I am afraid they cannot do very much. In all probability an example will be made of him."

CHAPTER XX

BITTER WATERS

Following Vera's suggestion, the next morning the five girls decided that they would spend the day in making the journey up the famous Mount Lowe, a few miles away. Afterwards they intended taking one of the long trail trips over the mountain, so that it would be impossible for them to return to their hotel until late afternoon.

For many reasons it seemed best that Mrs. Burton should be alone when she received the visit from Gerry. Surely Gerry would wish to have at least this first interview without interruption!

Believing it impossible that her guest could arrive before noon, Mrs. Burton spent the early hours of the morning in writing letters to her husband and sister, including several business notes as well. She would not confess it to herself; nevertheless she felt nervous over her first meeting with Gerry, for although only a few weeks had passed they had been crowded so tragically close with events in Gerry's life and in her own. There had been the unexpected tragedy of Billy's death, Billy who had been so unlike other boys in his life and in his final beautiful surrender of life.

Therefore when a knock came at her sitting-room door at some time between half-past ten and eleven, presuming one of the hotel servants was outside, Mrs. Burton said, "Come in," without raising her eyes from the paper upon which she was writing.

Afterwards the door opened softly and the next instant some one had entered the room, but instead of attending to whatever duty had made the intrusion necessary, the figure stood hesitating just inside the threshold.

After a little while, becoming vaguely conscious of this fact, Mrs. Burton glanced up.

"Gerry, you poor child!" she exclaimed with such sudden, warm sympathy and with such an utter lack of criticism or reproach that any human being would have been moved to gratitude and remorse.

Gerry stumbled forward. Poor Gerry, who had changed so completely in the past few weeks that even her delicate prettiness seemed to have vanished forever! She was so white and worn looking, so thin and unhappy.

"Then you forgive me?" she began.

Mrs. Burton took both her hands.

"We are not going to talk about forgiveness. You had your own life to live, Gerry, and it was natural that you should do the thing you supposed to be for your happiness without thinking of your gratitude or obligation to me. If it had been for your happiness I should not have expected you to think of me, although it would have been kinder of you. But of course, dear, when girls do reckless things, the reason older persons are grieved and angry is because of the consequences they are sure to bring upon themselves. Being young you cannot understand this! Yet it seems to me that you are having to pay rather more than other people. Do sit down, dear; the other girls have gone away for the day so we shall be entirely alone."

As if she were really too tired to stand, Gerry sank into the nearest chair.

"I am sorry; I have not been able to sleep since Felipe was arrested. I am told he keeps asking for me and I am not allowed to see him. He thinks he has done me a great injustice, but that is not true and besides I do not care."

Gerry spoke with entire self-forgetfulness.

"Mrs. Burton, I don't think you or perhaps anyone can understand, although I have tried to make Mr. Morris see. But Felipe and I have been perfectly miserable ever since we were married. Oh, it is not because we do not care for each other, because we do care very, very deeply! Only neither Felipe nor I seemed to realize the weakness and wrong of what we were doing until we were safely out of our own country and had time to face the truth. Then Felipe confessed to me he had been a coward. He seemed to think that no matter what happened in our future together, I must always think of him as a coward and compare him with other men who had done their duty. I don't know why he did not think of all this before. But Felipe has written me that he is almost glad he has been arrested. Anything which may happen to him will be better than having to live as a fugitive until the war is over. Besides, even afterwards, he could never look another American fellow in the face, remembering his own weakness! Can you understand how anyone could change a point of view so quickly, Mrs. Burton?" Gerry inquired wistfully. "It is hard even for me, and yet I realize that Felipe and I simply woke up from our selfish dream of happiness to realizing we had been traitors and cowards."

"I can understand almost any weakness and almost any strength in human beings, Gerry dear, after the years I have lived and the men and women I have known," Mrs. Burton answered, forgetting for the moment Gerry's youth. But the bitter waters of experience and regret having passed over Gerry, she was no longer young.

Suddenly Mrs. Burton got up and began walking up and down the room with the graceful impatience which was ever characteristic of her.

For a moment, watching her, Gerry felt her old charm so deeply that temporarily she forgot her own sorrow. The peculiar shining quality which Polly O'Neill had revealed as a girl in times of keen emotion she had never lost.

"I declare, Gerry, I cannot endure the thought that you and Felipe have so spoiled your lives at the age when you should have been happiest. If anything happens, if Felipe is kept in prison for a time, what do you intend to do?"

Gerry glanced down apparently at her hands which were lightly clasped together in her lap.

When she looked up at her companion she was smiling, even if somewhat tremulously.

"I am going to work, Mrs. Burton, although it may be difficult for you to believe after the effort I have made to escape even the thought of work. But

I think at last I have found something which will interest me. Mr. Morris is very kind; of course he must dislike me under the circumstances and feel I influenced Felipe, nevertheless he has asked me to live with him at the ranch indefinitely. But I won't do that, not after Felipe's trial is over. I shall do some kind of war work and I don't care now how menial or how humble it is. After a time perhaps I may learn to be useful. Felipe and I have talked things over and we want to do whatever is possible to atone for our mistake. If we only had it all to do over again! But then, of course, I realize what a foolish thing that is to say!"

"It may be foolish, Gerry, but it is universal."

After this remark Mrs. Burton did not sit down, nor did she speak again for several moments. Instead she stood, frowning and looking peculiarly determined and intense.

"Gerry, if Felipe were released from prison, do you think he would be willing to go into the army and do whatever he could to make himself a good soldier? I don't believe Felipe is a physical coward, he was merely a spiritual one. He is rash and impetuous and in a moment of actual fighting no one would be braver or perhaps more reckless. What he dreaded was the discipline, the thought of war, the having to relinquish the ease and beauty and pleasure of his daily life. Well, there must have been other boys like him, boys who fought with their own disinclination more gallantly than Felipe! Yet it would be foolish for the United States to lose a soldier for her army in order to gain a prisoner. Don't you think Mr. Morris and you also, Gerry, can persuade Felipe's judges to view the situation in this light? Let him accept whatever punishment they see fit to bestow, only they must not spoil his one chance of redeeming his mistake by fighting for his country."

Mrs. Burton might have been pleading with a court instead of addressing the solitary figure of one unhappy girl. However, she was merely thinking aloud.

"Mr. Morris is to make that plea for Felipe, although he has very little hope," Gerry answered. "Felipe would be willing to give even his life now to blot out the past."

Mrs. Burton walked over and placed her hands on Gerry's shoulders.

"My dear," she said, "I am going to stay here in California with you for a time at least and see what I can do to help. I may not have much influence, but I shall do my best. The girls can go home alone; they do not require me to chaperon them. I have no doubt they will have more pleasure in traveling without me. Besides, it seems to me that no one at present has the same need for me that you have, Gerry!"

Slowly in these past few weeks Gerry's soul had been coming to the light. The revelation of it now shone through her eyes, yet she made no effort to express her thanks in words.

"When the time arrives and Felipe is allowed to go to France to fight, perhaps I shall have learned to be useful. Do you think they will ever allow American girls to work behind the lines?"

Mrs. Burton shook her head.

"I don't know. Yet the call of France rings in all our ears and all our hearts today, Gerry. We can only answer the call when our opportunity arises."

The next volume in the Camp Fire series will deal with the work of the Camp Fire girls in France. They will establish Camp Fires among the young French girls. The old care-free days having passed away, they will also devote their energies to aiding the children of France and to doing "their bit" toward the restoration of that land of our affection, France, where, in the future as in the past, Beauty and Liberty must walk hand in hand. The title will be "The Camp Fire Girls on the Field of Honor."